GLIMPSES

A collection of 100 flash fiction stories that start out very short—

Frances Goodey

ISBN-13 978-0-646-89118-7

My special thanks to Queensland editor Lisa Toia for her meticulous editing skills.

The cover design is taken from an original work by Queensland artist Suzy Connelly.

I am delighted to dedicate my book to my mother, Merianne Connelly, who nurtured in me and my siblings a love of English and reading.

I thank my husband Ray for his support of my scribbling over many years.

I thank my daughters Deidre, Lisa, Suzy and Bernadette for their love and encouragement.

Now, isn't imagination a precious thing?

It peoples the earth with all manner of wonders…

Mark Twain

CONTENTS

STORIES WITH WORD COUNT 49-181

FINLEY

Little Gracie toddles over to Finley, the garden gnome. She puts a banana on a lettuce leaf in front of him, saying, 'You can have this, Finley,' and she kisses his nose. He's waited *forever* for a human kiss. She doesn't see Finley move but he's not there anymore.

49 words

THREATENING

'Your Instagram may be rife with retrograde memes,' the horoscope in the morning paper informed Emily and she gasped, 'Oh no!'

'What is it?' Reginald asked.

She told him and he said, 'Why are you upset about it?'

'I don't know what it means,' she replied worriedly, 'but it sounds so threatening!'

52 words

SAFETY

The sky was pumpkin yellow as the sun set, distant bushfires adding an extra dimension to the colour. The usual music of the magpies and curlews was missing to the dismay of the elves hiding under the biggest gum leaves; the birds must have flown away already.

But the head elf was worried. Would his magic be enough to transport them all to safety under this strangely-coloured sky?

68 words

GOOD ADVICE

'Those big ones, the humans, the ones who have to look after us, they are particularly deficient. They can do all kinds of amazing things but they are completely lacking the one thing that makes life worth living. What is it?'

Six soulful dark eyes looked at their mother. 'Our sense of smell!'

'What do you have to do to have a happy life?'

'Follow your nose,' they all barked.

70 words

MY GENIE

I've always wanted to go to Tajikistan, but my cat would miss me.

I'm thinking of asking my genie (who hates my cat) to swap with another genie for a while, one who'd let me take my cat to Tajikistan.

But I'm not hopeful. I've got my genie so tightly bound with super-strong spells, he won't do me any favours.

Tajikistan will have to wait until I don't have my cat any more.

Not that I'll let my genie know that.

81 words

VICTORIAN MYSTERY

'Go quickly now,' their mother said, 'but tread carefully on the polished stairs. You will find Granny's two flower baskets in the tall wardrobe in the back bedroom.'

In their pretty embroidered slippers, much too slippery for the highly polished stairs and too dainty for the uncarpeted rough wooden floors in the upper level, the girls hurried up the stairs.

Their mother found the two flower baskets on the floor in the back bedroom and the wardrobe doors shut firmly.

Of the two girls there was no sign. Ever.

89 words

DO NOT APPROACH

'The rumenilo's escaped,' BioSecurity announced. 'The blushing creature. Report if seen. Do not approach.'

Rossman's stomach churned as he locked the children in.

The alien looked like a teddy bear, and blushing as prettily as it did any child would pick it up.

Even hard-headed Rossman had admired the rumenilo's pulsing pattern of flushing and paling, as appealing as a lover's blush. It was cute but so dangerous—it had killed every test animal placed near it. Invisibly. They had no idea about its anatomy or anything else.

And it was out in the ship.

95 words

THE RETURN

Mrs Spangerley erupted through her front door screaming. The neighbours on each side scrambled from their houses in alarm, holding her, trying to calm her down, trying to find out what was wrong.

Mr Spangerley came out from the house looking spick and span as usual, holding his little daughter's hand. The neighbours turned from Mrs Spangerley, who by now was quietly sobbing, to stare at the little girl. Her hair was clearly elflock: her eyes were invisible behind the masses of tangled hair.

'Elves!' the neighbours whispered to each other. 'The elves are back!'

95 words

SURVIVAL

Back in the 2060s when the climate appeared to be settling into its new pattern—fewer droughts, more regular rainy seasons—it was discovered that many of the larger wild animals were vanishing at an increasing rate. That was when the German scientist Wolfgang Dietrich announced he had perfected a way to miniaturise large animals.

The miniature pet elephant, only 12cm tall, that his family were raising convinced the world that miniaturisation was the way to go. Everyone could have a pet elephant, or a back yard (well fenced) of wild savage animals.

What could go wrong?

97 words

THE REAL STORY

The television reporter was clearly trying not to smile as he said the words, 'The wolf has been found not guilty!'

It turned out that the wolf had been tricked by Red Riding Hood who admitted in court that she knew the wolf was following her all the time.

She had contacted her friend Petunia Pig who agreed with Red's plan. When the wolf slipped into Grandma's house, Petunia was already in Grandma's bed, in Grandma's nightie and mob cap.

The jury decided that since pigs are the natural prey of wolves, there had been no crime.

97 words

TREES

The children stood at the high fence gazing in through the wire at the trees.

They could see birds flitting in and out of the trees, the wind making the branches sway and leaves falling to the ground.

They turned their backs on the scene to survey the landscape they had walked through to this point. There were no trees out there.

The only trees in the whole area were here, behind the wire fence with its sign: TREE PROTECTION ZONE—DO NOT DISTURB.

The younger boy said, 'My dad says he used to climb them, once.'

97 words

NO ONE KNOWS

Shelagh froze, head bowed, hands in the suds. 'Tell me again.'

Rowan, quietly, sheepishly, 'We rigged the vote.'

Rowena, a head taller and brazen in her defiance, declared, 'I did it! I couldn't let that creep—'

Rowan interrupted, 'Ma, you know Dad will make the best King's Protector.'

Shelagh raised her eyes from the sink to the window. A coach was stopping, its door emblazoned with the emblem of the Fae Court.

'We were careful with the magic, Ma,' Rowena went on. 'No one knows. We were so meticulous, Ma.'

Shelagh turned to memorise her beloved, foolish, children's faces.

100 words

HISTORY

The rather odd-looking man in red framed spectacles went from newsagent to newsagent asking for a tabloid. Of course there was not even one to be found in this digital age.

When he told the third newsagent what he wanted, the woman behind the counter asked why.

'I want the results of a competition that was held yesterday, a shooting competition. My cousin was in the pistol-shooting section.'

He happened to glance at a display of calendars nearby and quickly excused himself. If he wanted a tabloid souvenir of his great-great-grandfather's shooting prowess, he'd have to travel back another 20 years.

101 words

QUICK EXIT

The skinny worker wiped sweat from his brow, tossed his worn jacket over one shoulder, picked up his spade and turned away from the hole he had so industriously dug.

The sun was setting and he cursed quietly. He should have finished earlier.

With firm and precise steps he strode towards the cemetery's exit, carefully not looking in the direction of the figures rising through the grass, through the gravesites, oozing out of the vaults scattered here and there. Silently they ambled, plodded, shambled and lumbered behind him, but as usual they were too slow to reach him before he walked through the gate.

104 words

MEETING

The puppy got to its feet and promptly fell down. Its rolls of fat jiggled as it stood again, this time staying upright. It paused, turned its head and stared as a small boy, somewhat pale and transparent, seeped through the living room wall. He glided across the carpet and bent to touch the pup on its head but before the cold barely-there finger could reach the pup, it squealed and tried hard to scuttle backward.

Laughing, the living warm-blooded tiny girl grabbed the pup, holding it firmly, too firmly, and it squealed again and its legs scrabbled against her.

The ghostly boy sadly vanished back into the wall.

109 words

INEXPLICABLE

The letters DNA were written in enormous letters above the doorway into the zombies exhibit. One might think they referred to a scientific session of some kind, but they meant DO NOT APPROACH.

The intelligent among those fortunate enough to survive the convulsions knew not to go anywhere near the zombies, avoiding even glancing at the poor unfortunates on display.

The ignorant among them occasionally risked everything, wandering among the more gruesome exhibits, their chocolate ice creams oozing stickiness despite the air conditioning, enjoying the rush of cool air in the heat.

Standing too close.

One or two of the attendants were tempted to leave them to it.

The way some people simply forgot about the zombie apocalypse was just inexplicable.

121 words

SCRATCHES

There were scratches on the wall and they puzzled the real estate agent. The house was pristine, apart from the scratches low on the external wall of the kitchen.

She only noticed them because the tiny toddler of the couple viewing the house tried to climb in through the swinging pet door and the scratches were alongside the door.

Later she learned that the next-door neighbours' old blind dog had been a frequent visitor to the house, and when the pet door wouldn't open, it would scratch at the wall and the door.

The scratches were clearly recent—the new paint had been gouged—but the neighbours had been gone for years and their blind dog had been dead even longer.

121 words

POSITIVITY

The young would-be witch looked at the instructions her mentor had provided and felt unsure. She took a deep breath—uncertainty and doubt would undermine her more quickly than anything else. Remembering her mindfulness techniques, she closed her eyes. Another deep breath and she was ready.

First, create a song of gratitude. Her mind filled with the music of the new song, and she had to persuade the water bubbling along in the little creek to be her friend. She had to spell a patch of still water in the moving stream to bear her weight.

She began humming her new song and crossed her fingers. Uh-oh! Crossing your fingers for good luck was a sign of doubt.

She shook her fingers, humming, and stepped onto the creek.

128 words

NIGHT WORK

The old monk carefully placed his feet on the wicker matting as he turned into the abbey library. He'd become a bit unsteady lately and he was truly concerned about falling and dropping the old oil lamp. A fire would be disastrous among the ancient books and manuscripts.

He reached his desk and positioned the oil lamp in a safe spot and turned to pull out the chair. His work from last night was waiting.

Voices sounded in the corridor he'd so recently traversed and two young monks entered the room. One of them flicked a switch near the door and the old monk winced as light filled the room from overhead.

The other young monk said, 'I could swear I smell old lamp oil in this room sometimes.'

129 words

SANDY FIND

She bent to pick up a half-buried seashell. She brushed at the sand, not yet wanting to dig her fingers around it, and a rounded pearly grey surface appeared. Intrigued, she did thrust her fingers down, and pulled. A narrow oblong object with rounded ends emerged from the sand, made entirely of a pearlised almost mother-of-pearl material, not plastic she could tell: it was too translucent.

It had a dark ring about two centimetres from one end, inviting to be turned. She did so and a glow appeared at the opening, and a trembling susurrus of sound began.

With a gulp, she tightened the top, knelt to dig a hole in the sand and pushed it deep into the hole.

Then she kicked sand over it and walked away.

129 words

THE MERMAID

The cake on its stand had a single candle and the tiny boy stood staring at it. He turned to his great grandfather and said, 'Have you forgotten you should have all your numbers on the cake?'

The old fellow leaned over and said, 'Eighty-eight candles wouldn't fit.' He sat back and gazed at the cake. 'Do you like the lady on the top?'

'That's not a lady, that's a mermaid,' the boy said scornfully. 'Anyway, why do you have a mermaid on your cake?'

'She's splendid, isn't she?' the old man said, not answering him. The boy turned away.

The old man knew the boy wouldn't understand his tale of nearly drowning once after a horrific ferry foundering in Asian waters, when a mermaid kept him afloat.

Others reckoned they'd seen a dolphin, but he knew what he knew.

140 words

SUNSET

The scene in front of Todd was so picturesque that just about everyone nearby was snapping images of it. The river making its way between the darkening shadowy hills reflected the pink and gold sky above in an amazing palette of colour. An owl hooting in the trees behind him made him smile.

Todd wasn't taking static images; he had a video camera recording the sun setting, capturing the sights and the sounds. It was a shame he couldn't capture the smells, he thought.

He had at least twenty movies saved of sunrises and sunsets and he had friends and family filming more. When he was settled and surviving on Mars, surrounded by the dry red of its soil, the only sound caused by wind stirring the arid sands, he wanted to experience again this sunset in all its glory. And to hear the owl.

145 words

A NEW SKILL

After the alien craft departed Earth, its leader saying they would never return, some people discovered they had received a parting gift. It was a new ability in mathematical figuring. The new facility in understanding mathematics of all kinds was an extreme shock because it became clear that many of the people who were now conversant with mathematics had never had an interest in maths at all.

One of the sudden experts had been known to challenge a teacher to explain exactly why two plus two had to equal four.

Where some people had once had difficulty adding figures together, or subtracting and dividing them, now Fibonacci sequences and coefficients were as child's play; now they could multiply, double, and triple as never before. But now, also, to the wonder of many mathematicians, they could yuple, an alien way of mathematising that no one on Earth understood at all.

149 words

THE WEDNESDAY MELODY

I'm sorry, I can't explain the scientific reasoning behind what happened. I could only follow it by reading the news reports which were fairly complex—they had to dumb it down for general readers like me with no scientific bent and less knowledge of music.

I like music—who doesn't?—but I can't sing in tune and I certainly can't read music. So when I'm told that maths and music have a special relationship and that explains the melody that arrived nearly forty years ago from outer space—well, I guess I trust the science. As you know, the Wednesday Melody permeates damn near everything (pardon my French). Films. Ads. Politics. Music. Charming as it is, I'm sick of it.

It's called 'the Wednesday melody' because it arrived on a Wednesday.

To sum it up: signals arrived in maths form which translated to musical notes that made a melody.

Now there's a new set of maths signals. That means a new melody, the 'Friday melody'. The scientists say that whoever is transmitting it is closer to Earth.

Much, much closer.

180 words

Frances Goodey

VISITING

‘This is a park, you know what a park is?’

‘I’ve read about them. Is it safe to be here? Won’t the natives discover us?’

‘They’re called humans, little one. No, they won’t discover us. They see our ship but it looks like part of the park. Look, child, see this clear glass that shows our images? It is called a mirror. What do you see?’

‘Natives! I mean, humans! But it’s us! I look so ... strange. Two eyes. It’s so strange.’

‘This is what the humans see when they look at us. They think they are alone in the universe, but as long as they keep on providing these fun rides—look up there, how high it is!’

‘Let’s go on it. Oh look, there’s my classmate and his dad. They look normal to me. Are you sure the humans can’t see us as we are?’

‘Smile at this female. Spread your mouth parts, show your teeth to her. It’s okay. See what happens.’

‘Oh, she patted my antennae.’

‘She couldn’t see them. Let’s go on this high ride.’

181 words

STORIES WITH WORD COUNT 194-294

VERY LIKE EARTH

The commander and his crew had been waiting for what seemed like hours, eager for the fog to lift. The atmosphere had been sampled at various points above the vast ocean and it was supremely suitable for humans. It was almost identical to earth's atmosphere. But it was covered in a shifting roiling fog.

That layer of rolling mist or fog was frustrating. Above the clouds, up where they were, the local sun was very like earth's. The fog that covered the one and only island on this planet seemed to be the same fog that covered the ocean and their penetrating radar and sonar showed the island had a plentiful cover of plant life.

The exploratory team reported they could see barely a metre in front of them. They did not dare to separate, to explore widely, even though the air was pleasant, if damp with the fog.

Every time it was over the hidden island, the orbiting ship's sensors picked up the hidden team moving down below and heard: 'the fog is not lifting' and 'we still can't see what's here'.

Until the latest orbit when there was no sign of life.

194 words

SNOWGULL

The little creature lying on the corridor floor was distressed, its breathing fast and frantic. John and I stared at it, reluctant to help although it was so helpless. It was alien. Not a bird, not a mammal; its lush fur, or feathers, it was hard to tell, surrounded its body shape like a cloud, pale grey shot through with lightning-colours like paint splashes. Fur maybe, I thought, watching as John hovered his hand tentatively above it.

'I'd love to run my fingers through it, just to see what it feels like,' he said, 'but it's a snowgull. Escaped from the zoo zone I guess.'

He stood and we both moved back a step. People claimed snowgulls exuded a poisonous vapour and I'd read their body temperature was so low that humans could freeze just from touching them. Like that island coast on that last planet, where five people died just from breathing the unfiltered air. It was technically fit for humans, but so cold one breath could kill.

The tiles under the little snowgull were icing up and its breathing was slowing. John said, 'I'll call the zoo.' It was only one corridor away but a call would be quicker since we couldn't pick it up.

207 words

THE RIGHT MAN

Rosalie had always known she was different from other people. She'd always been able to sense what other people were feeling—not their thoughts or ideas, just how they were really feeling. Talking to someone who was quite civil and apparently perfectly friendly but at the same time seething with anger, or trying to deal with deep distress, or simply itching to get away, made life very difficult for Rosalie.

Inevitably she became somewhat isolated, choosing a lifestyle that kept her away from other people.

She'd been unable to keep boyfriends. Men initially attracted to her looks were sooner or later put off by her pinpoint accuracy in knowing what they really felt. About her, about politics, about sport, about other people, it didn't matter. Rosalie couldn't be deceived.

One day, entering an empty alcove in the city library, she had the eerie sense that someone was nearby. Invisible.

She couldn't resist calling out, 'Who's there?' and was astounded when a man materialised in front of her. He smiled and she returned the smile. He was tall, and quite handsome, with curly hair and bright brown eyes. But it wasn't his looks that made her smile at him.

She couldn't sense what he was feeling! Nothing at all. Maybe she'd found the man for her at last. If he were human.

221 words

WAITING

The children went quietly, their mother pressing them from behind, their father hanging back, looking into the space outside the cave, tempted.

Their mother called to him, 'If the science is right, if all light disappears and people go crazy and wreck everything, how will we survive without you?'

He turned then and followed her. Followed his wife and his three children who by now were excitedly catching up to their friends, deep in the deepest part of the cavernous space. The mothers clustered together for a time, then separated to sort out lanterns, bedding and food. They'd been told to prepare for at least a few days' stay.

If the scientists were right, all three suns would darken, or disappear, the sky would turn dark and there would be no sunlight. It seemed impossible of course, but they were prepared. But, never had there been no light! It was laughable to think the sky could darken!

Imagine! One of the scientists had translated a mysterious word from ancient writing, 'morning', to mean 'the return of light'. That was supposed to suggest the suns would darken but only for a time, and at least one sun would shine again and the darkness would be banished.

So here they were, deep in a cave in darkness rarely experienced, waiting for this thing called *morning*.

With apologies to Isaac Asimov and his 'Nightfall' .

223 words

Frances Goodey

A FLEETING GLIMPSE

'Wait!' Scowling, Harry stood in the doorway, hands on hips.

The three boys promptly shut up but Wayne took a step forward, saying 'Dad,' fervour clear in his voice, but Harry's upraised finger stopped him.

'In a sec, Wayne. All of you, pick up your bikes. Wayne's mum is due home any minute and she'll run over them.'

Bikes restored to order, Wayne's excited words erupted. 'Dad, you won't believe it but it's true! We were riding past the Johnson's north paddock and we saw this UFO. It lifted up from the middle of the paddock. We were all up on our bikes and saw it!'

'There, just in time,' Harry said, interrupting the other boys' echoes of Wayne's claim and pointing as his wife's car turned into the driveway. The boys turned to look. As they did, Harry said in a hushed voice, 'You've gotta be kidding me!' and the boys swung back.

Harry's trembling finger was pointing into the sky at a round saucer-shaped machine or plane or device or whatever the hell it was.

His wife called, 'What's up, fellas?' and she looked in the same direction, catching a fleeting glimpse of the UFO as it whizzed straight up, did a sharp turn and disappeared over the cane fields.

No one said anything for a while, but Wayne was deeply satisfied. Seeing a UFO was fantastic, but it was great that he'd seen it before his dad did.

241 words

FAREWELL TO AGNES

'The horses don't get sick, do they, Grandad?' the little boy asked as they watched Wymond and Rufus lift Agnes's wasted body into the back of the cart. Rufus was coughing, a wet sound that had him hunched, and gasping through his makeshift mask. The stench of death permeated the air, and both boy and old man kept a hand over their noses and their mouths.

'That's good noticin', young Elric,' Herry, the old man, said. 'Cats don't, neither, that's why we'll keep Missy Sharpclaws.' He patted the black cat's head while the boy held her close. 'I reckon cats are good to have around, keep the rats and mice away. I hope she'll stay with us all the time now.'

They watched the cart taking away the cat's owner. Agnes had been a good neighbour and Herry didn't believe for a minute that she was a witch. If she was a witch, she wouldn't have got the plague, would she?

'Didn't do Agnes any good, having the cat,' the boy muttered.

'That's because the cat spends all its time with you, you young scamp!'

They went inside, hoping the plague would pass them by. The plague had taken Maud, Elric's mother, and his two sisters. Elric's dad, the Scotsman who had won Maud's heart over Herry's objections, died last.

Herry shut the door, shutting out the world, and he rubbed his grandson's back fondly as the boy and the cat nestled close.

243 words

DEADLY SANDALWOOD

No human being ever discovered that Earth had been invaded. No one ever realised that a seemingly insignificant moment in a department store saved all humanity.

That moment was the instant that Maryanne Tomlinson decided on a nebulising diffuser rather than an ultrasonic diffuser.

Had Maryanne bought the ultrasonic version which would send her beloved essential oils into the air using the ultrasonic vibrations caused to the water in it, the room would have smelt delightful of course, depending on the essential oil used (Maryanne loved the aroma of sandalwood, at least for a short time) but it would also have humidified the air.

The too-small-to-see aliens that floated through Maryanne's living room window (not yet provided with the insect screen waiting in her garage) would have really enjoyed the dampness imparted by the ultrasonic vibrations (caused by the electricity the device was plugged into).

But, and it's a very big but, Maryanne decided on the waterless nebulising diffuser which dispersed her essential oils significantly faster than an ultrasonic diffuser, and at a higher concentration.

The poor tiny aliens only just managed a mangled message to their colleagues awaiting word just the other side of Mars, a message which conveyed the intelligence that Earth's atmosphere was inimical to them. Go elsewhere! Do not follow us! Farewell forever!

The poor tiny aliens copped a faceful and skinful and lungful of sandalwood essential oil molecules unmediated by water, and expired in very short order.

The world owes Maryanne Tomlinson a huge debt.

250 words

NEIGHBOURS

The new neighbours arrive wearing huge hats, long sleeves, enormous sunglasses. All of them. Inside, after they remove the hats and sunglasses, the mother hands me her party offering (mm, empanadas, harissa yoghurt, spanakopita pinwheels).

'Our whole family are photophobic,' she says, 'allergic to sunlight and, sadly, we're all allergic to garlic as well.'

I think, '*Empanadas without garlic! She must be kidding*!' In due course I discover the empanadas are store-bought so there's no lack of garlic.

Intrigued at the thought of both parents and both teenaged boys being, what was it, *photophobic*, I ask one of the boys about it. He looks so uncomfortable trying to find something to say that I take pity on him. I pat him on the shoulder and say, 'It's okay, we all have our oddities, don't we?' and laugh.

He's gazing at my hand, and I become uncomfortable in turn. He looks up at me and smiles. There's something odd about his teeth but his words distract me. 'You have such beautiful skin,' he says, quite boldly I think for a teenage boy speaking to a mature woman. 'May I?' And he takes my hand. He turns it over and runs his fingers over my inner wrist. 'Your fair skin shows your veins really clearly, doesn't it?'

How can a teenager seem so creepy? What an odd boy! He gazes at me and releases my hand. He turns away and I do too, gladly.

I find myself looking at those veins now and again.

252 words

SABOTAGE

As they approached the chosen landing site, Ella thought back to the frightening message they'd had from Houston.

Headquarters had learned something regrettable about the module and Hank and Ella should advise immediately of anything abnormal occurring. Houston wouldn't get the message for 35 minutes, but at least they would be aware.

A subcontractor involved in designing and creating the outer shell of their landing module had learned that one of their group is a cultist who believes humans should stay on Earth. The man had confessed to sabotaging one of the formulas that created the new materials used in forming the module.

Ella had looked around her. Everything worked, communications with Earth had gone ok, they could breathe. So far. Now here they were, about to land on the planetoid and not talking about the nutty saboteur.

The landing went so smoothly that Ella relaxed, putting her fears aside.

Three hours later they were suited up and about to do a repeat of Neil Armstrong's famous stepping onto another planetary body when there was an eerie crackling sound. It surrounded them as if coming from the walls of the module. It lasted about 20 seconds.

Hank and Ella looked at each other, their eyes wide inside their helmets. Hank spluttered, 'It sounds like it's cooling off!'

'Cooling off? It's not supposed to cool off!' Ella's heart thumped and Hank swore.

They looked around fearfully and stared at each other. The crackling came again and didn't stop as together they reached for the radio.

254 words

ANNIVERSARY

The two little girls ran back to their mother leaving the boy strolling with their dad. Weather permitting, once a month the family went for a moonwalk. They ambled along looking at the full moon shining down on them.

'Can you believe that a hundred years ago, in 2021, no one really expected men would leave the Earth to live on another planetary body. It's an amazing accomplishment.'

'And now it's the anniversary,' the boy said. 'We've been living up there for 20 years.'

'Hmm,' his dad said. 'My grandparents were alive when we first stepped on the moon.'

'That's a long time ago,' the boy said. 'Why did it take so long to go back?'

'Politics, usually.' He chuckled at the boy's expression, clear in the moon's glow. 'Mother Nature got in the way. You've learned about the extremes of climate. Food shortages. Sea levels rose. Islands and coastlines disappeared, people moved inland—what people were left after floods and fires. And—' he paused to rumple his boy's hair fondly, 'fewer children were born. We've had a hundred years of recovery.' He took a breath. What a dreary litany.

'But now we're back up there, maybe you will go yourself one day.'

'Maybe,' the boy said. 'But I'd rather go to Mars.'

'I remember my grandfather saying that!' his dad exclaimed.

'I hope we get there before *I'm* a grandfather!' the boy said, laughing.

Thinking about the problems of human survival in space, his dad didn't have the heart to say, 'Don't hold your breath, son.'

258 words

CHRISTMAS BOND

When Sam Lowood was eight years old, in 1953, he sat on Santa's lap in the big store and found he couldn't remember what he was going to ask for. That's why he was there, right? To tell Santa what he wanted for Christmas?

Sam had heard rumours about Santa not being real but so far had managed to push the thought away. Sitting on the big man's knee, looking into his eyes, Sam felt a bond with Santa that both thrilled and puzzled him, almost an electrical connection between their eyes, or their brains, or something.

Sam was science minded and could almost make sense of the idea of electricity between two people, even if one was Santa.

From Santa's point of view, Sam really had connected. At Sam's age, or fairly close to it, this Santa (whose name had once been Josiah Templeton) had seen the Santa of his time clearly enough through an opaque crown glass window and felt that same connection. That was more than 120 years ago and Santa was extremely happy, in 1953, to have come across Sam.

For Sam, it was electricity. For the old Santa, it had been magic.

Sam forgot about this encounter of course. He grew up, and played Santa for his own children, and for his grandchildren, and sometimes at Christmas parties for other adults.

But Sam Lowood would remember this 1953 moment during his 76th year when he would be given a choice: become Santa until another young boy connected with him, sometime in the future. Or die. Today.

261 words

BEING THERE

'I remember it so clearly,' I heard myself say, lying with my eyes closed. The ceiling fan soothed me with its regular swish.

'Tell me more,' the calm voice instructed, and I sighed, feeling tension ease away.

'I'd crept away from my mum who was back in the bush with my baby brother, feeding him. I followed the men who were going to the beach. I knew my dad would let me play in the little waves and maybe my uncles would take me in the deep water but when I caught up to them they were standing very still. I had to look between their legs and their spears and I could see a big ship out in the water but three little boats had pulled up on the sand. Strange beings were getting out of them. My mob were murmuring and I was frightened. The new people were ghosts. Their skin was white and their eyes were the colour of the sky and they didn't wear kangaroo skin or wallaby skin; their skins were many colours.'

I could hear my voice change. 'I was afraid of the ghosts and I ran back to my mother. She didn't believe me about the ghosts at first. That day the ghosts went away in their boats, but some time later, when I was a young mother myself, they returned. This time they stayed forever in our land.'

I could feel tears seeping down my cheeks, and the hypnotist touched my hand, saying what she needed to say to bring me back to myself.

262 words

WORDS OF UNDOING

'Godwin, the human? Mr Grumpy?'

Gran Rainyrose sighed. 'I am dying, Snowlily, and I empower you to undo the curse I inflicted on him when he was young. Godwin unknowingly kicked me one day and I cursed him to joylessness. He became a horrid man and I regret it. I should have removed the curse long ago.' She sighed again. 'Your task is to make Godwin Bolam happy,' Gran Rainyrose Blossom said to the young fairy. 'I give you permission to achieve that task by any means you can.'

She whispered a few words and waved Snowlily away.

At Godwin's cottage. Snowlily chanted the words of undoing, throwing in words of joy and laughter. He had been unhappy a long time!

Godwin started laughing. Chortling, giggling, chuckling, cackling. He left the house heading to the village, laughing, giggling to himself. Sometimes it was a hearty booming laugh, sometimes just happy giggling. Every now and then he halted, bent by his laughter. He could not stop.

Snowlily flew behind the laughing man, horror-struck. She didn't like what she had done. He was an old man, stumbling along, nearly falling, laughing, giggling. She wrung her hands, almost in tears.

Snowlily thought quickly. Laughter alone was not happiness. And by any means, Gran Rainyrose had said. Snowlily flew over Godwin's head and, floating, appeared in front of him. She stopped his giggling and he took deep breaths and stared at her.

She told him what Gran Rainyrose had done to him, and he frowned. He looked so fierce!

'What would make you happy, Mr Grum—Godwin?'

263 words

SPECIAL GUESTS

Jake's voice was tense when he asked me, for the third time, 'Are you sure the bedrooms are all dark enough? Are the rooms really prepared for them?'

'Yes, Jake, I'm sure. New blackout curtains, new mattresses that are rock hard, half a dozen blankets of different weights. I'm sure the family will be comfortable.'

He patted my shoulder then threw an arm around me. 'Thanks, love, for taking this all so calmly. It's not every day we get visitors who are so strange.'

I smiled at him. 'It's probably a bit like having Amish guests. You change your rooms to suit them, so they'll be comfortable. Even though they must expect things will be different from home.'

We settled on the couch to wait for the coach bringing Jake's brother Tim and his wife Rosemary. They had seven-year-old Adam with them. Adam was born in the settlement, not the first by a long shot, but settlement-born meant he'd be freaking out by the time he reached us. They lived underground, deep, deep underground, only rarely venturing to the surface. Never seeing a blue sky, green grass, brown earth. Rain. Water running in gutters. Fresh air. Enough to freak out anyone who'd never experienced these things.

They will be so pale, with absolutely no exposure to sunlight. Adam particularly.

When Jake and Rosemary volunteered to spend their lives on Mars, I thought we'd never see them again but things had gone so well the settlers were able to have short holidays back here.

The twins came scampering into the room, both yelling. 'The Martians are here, the Martians are here!'

270 words

SILENCE

People might think that life on board the International Space Station is a quiet undertaking, but they'd be wrong. There are the mechanical sounds of machines and devices operating as they should, such as converting humid breaths to liquid water, constant communications between those on board and back on earth, the pumping sounds as machines keep the conditions safe for humans. Safe too for the animals and plants undergoing experimentation. And there are voices—accents varying over the years: American, Russian, Indian, Australian, Japanese.

32-year-old Bella Simpson once read about the living conditions aboard the ISS. Like a 'terrible share house' one can't get away from, with smells and noises—just an incredible mess that's packed with dead skin cells and crumbs. And no one gets a decent sleep.

Bella was thrilled at having her first spacewalk, sharing a repair job on the outer shell of the station with old hand Chris Patton. The two talked easily to each other on their two-way link and with those on the station. And in the background of those brief chats were the constant everyday noises: pumps, machines, voices.

Until the time came when those noises were not there. The voices were not there. The link to the station was gone. Their link to Earth was gone. And then, abruptly, the link to each other was gone.

For Bella and Chris, the only sound was their own breathing. And when each of them held a breath momentarily, hoping beyond hope to hear another sound, a voice, a pump, a mouse's squeak from the lab, when they held their breath, there was only deathly silence.

271 words

Frances Goodey

FUTURE PLANS

'I've decided to write my essay on time travel,' 17-year-old Travis said to his parents at dinner between forkfuls of pasta. 'My last-ever essay at high school,' he added. 'I can hardly believe it.'

His parents glanced at each other. Both scientists, they loved the fact that their only son was a budding scientist too, but—

'Time travel?' said his father, frowning, putting down his fork, while his mother raised her eyebrows and stared at him. 'You can't write fiction in an essay!'

'It's okay,' Travis assured them. 'It won't be fiction. Don't worry. I know it's the right thing to do.'

'What do you mean? How can you know it's the right thing to do?' His mother was beginning to worry. Year 12 was such a strain on the kids. This sounded weird.

'The essay will pave the way for me to get into the right university and work on the techniques and technology needed for real time travel.'

Again, his parents glanced at each other. Was their son losing it?

'You'd better explain,' his father said sternly, pushing his dinner aside.

'I don't expect you to believe me, but last night I had a brief visit from my future self. He said to do the essay, and not to forget to include my theory about the folding of spacetime.'

His parents just stared at him.

'You just have to fold it,' he shrugged, turning back to his dinner. 'He told me how. I'll put it in the essay, or hint at it anyway. I'll complete the work before I'm 24, win the Nobel and change the world.'

He started eating.

272 words

SPINNERS

It was when we were hiking through Bhutan last year, you know the short trip away that we had, the boys and I? Well, I know you've heard us say it was a fairytale trip, absolutely everything went right.

The weather was perfect, the scenery to die for, the mountains not too tough, the people were great, so welcoming.

We even lucked into a once-in-ten-year parade by an offshoot of the main religious group, some kind of exotic belief system. The parade was devoted to their god, or goddess, hard to tell under the exotic mask and the all-enveloping robes, but I think it was a child under the mask, in a golden carriage. Could have been a very short adult.

There was a circle of little people surrounding the carriage, I'm sure they were adults, dwarfs maybe, plump like dumplings, dimples in fat cheeks, solid, squat little figures, also dressed in colourful robes, but no masks. They were hard to see, actually; they were spinning around as they walked beside and behind the god-figure, almost bumping into the carriage. As they went, they were throwing something over the roof of the carriage to each other, the spinning figures making amazing catches. Woven balls, something like that, each catch a breathtaking miracle. Hard enough to keep going in a straight line while you spin, let alone catch a ball consistently!

It was almost dusk when we watched that magnificent parade go by. It was captivating. But it turned out to be weird too. One of the little spinning people caught my eye and winked at me.

The boys told me later they didn't see any little people at all, throwing balls or otherwise.

283 words

Frances Goodey

PHONING

Marcie tapped the right edge of her jaw to end the call. She sighed. If only Mum would have the comm chips installed. They were so tiny, one on the left side to start a call, one on the right to end it. But no, Mum had to have a telephone she could hold and talk into.

Marcie closed the computer. That was work done for the day. Now, it was her turn to cook. She had to smile, as she set about preparing dinner, seeing Ronnie's special box on a bench. The words 'phone box' were written on it in big black letters. Trust him to take to his Gran's bright idea.

'You can make your own phone, you know,' Ronnie's Gran had told him a few days before. 'All you need is two empty tin cans and a long piece of string.'

'A home-made telephone!' Ronnie had scoffed. Later he'd told his mother he thought Gran was losing it, so in the interests of family unity Marcie had suggested he try.

With his brother still a baby, Ronnie called on Greta next door, who was a year younger, to be co-opted into his scientific experiment.

After much trial and error, it worked beautifully. With Ronnie on the lowest branch of a tree in his back yard and Greta on her back verandah and the string straight and taut between the two cans, words flew back and forth, once they learned to coordinate speaking and listening.

Marcie smiled, peeling veggies. Ronnie planned to take his phone-in-a-box to school.

What a world! From two cans and a piece of string to a handheld phone with a keypad, to 'touch your jaw and phone anyone'!

284 words

WITNESSES

'I can't take another step, husband,' the weary woman whispered. The donkey she had just seen vanish into the darkness of the stable brayed loudly, glad to be relieved of the burden of the heavily pregnant woman.

The man tightened his grip around her waist and the innkeeper's wife beckoned them in further.

'There's more room here,' she said to the man, 'than in a tiny room at the back of the inn. It's certainly much quieter with all the travellers coming here to register for the census.'

He looked around the stable. It was clean enough, as stables go; the few animals were quiet, staring in an unsettlingly direct way.

'We can lie the baby on the small manger's hay,' the woman said, throwing a cloth over it, 'and this,' she added, shaking out a large bed-sized woven cloth, 'your wife will be comfortable on.' She threw it over a bed of hay slightly raised off the floor. Probably a farmhand slept there, he thought.

The sounds coming from his wife as the woman settled her prickled the back of his neck. He stepped aside, a few paces back. The women wouldn't want a man close right now.

A flicker in the lamplight caught his attention briefly but he ignored it, bowing his head and praying to his god that all would be well with his wife and his baby.

No one noticed the many presences above and around the birthing bed. No one knew that unseen folk had travelled far to be here, following ley lines from all around the world. The angels, sentinels of the unseen, already had their turn—with the shepherds.

Here, tonight, it was the tiniest folk who would witness this godly birth.

289 words

Frances Goodey

WARNINGS

I've just had my tenth birthday and I've met my husband. I knew I would, I've known for years. But it was a shock too—he's so old! And he's too tall! He says I'll grow much taller.

But what made it special, meeting him for the first time, was that he told me about my secret. No one knows it but him. He wants to warn me.

When you're in the witching world, you know what people can do. Witches. Some make light, some make fire, some can fly, some read minds, some do true magic and make it look like a performance. When you grow up in a family of witches, you learn to hide your talents from ordinary people and you keep lots of secrets.

When I grow up, I'm going to marry Harrison and we're going to be really rich and start up lots of charities, helping ordinary people.

Harrison told me that on my 18th birthday, my talent will reveal itself. He's travelled back in time to tell me. That's his talent, travelling back in time. Other witches do it too. Travel back.

When I turn 18, I am going to be able, suddenly, to travel forward in time. The first witch ever to do it.

I will only be able to go two days ahead, always just the day after tomorrow, but that's enough to have winning Lotto tickets, place bets on sports (Harrison loves doing that, he told me—how boring!), and get rich from other things called stocks and shares.

I will warn people about coming dangers.

But I have to do it secretly or I'll end up in government hands. That's what Harrison says. It sounds scary.

Don't tell anyone, will you?

291 words

HAPPY NEW YEAR!

New Year's Eve, 2044. Another eight months, a bit less, and I'll be a century old. I look at myself in the mirror. Craggy wrinkles make me look like my oldest uncle who was born in the last year of the 1800s. If *he* were alive, he'd be 144! Ha! He'd be a medical miracle!

I grimace at the wrinkles but notice my eyes still look clear—thank goodness my genetic inheritance didn't include cataracts. Poor vision maybe, but clear eyes.

One of my great-grandsons asked me today if I might get a message from the king when I have my hundredth birthday. I told him it wasn't likely. The king will be turning 100 himself in three years—he's only three years younger than me but he's gaga, poor fellow. He had to wait for ages to become king, then only a few years later he was tucked away out of sight as his mind went. Apparently, according to the magazines, he's healthy, just lost to the world with dementia.

His sons and grandsons, and granddaughters of course, must be impatient with the poor man.

He was unlucky in his genetic inheritance. His father and mother and grandmother all lived to ripe old ages, like him, but they kept their wits to the end.

Oh well. I count my blessings. I might be covered in wrinkles from my scalp to the soles of my feet, but my mind is wrinkle-free. And I have a lovely bunch of young relations who love me and look after me.

I'll try to hang on till my birthday. How exciting to have three digits in my age! In the meantime, as this could be my last ever New Year's Eve, I will enjoy the celebration. Happy 2044!

294 words

STORIES WITH WORD COUNT 318-482

CONSPIRACY

My cousin Miranda and I hadn't seen each other for a year, pandemic and personality being the main reasons.

'I've left Dan until he gets vaccinated,' she'd announced at the door.

She added as she came into the living room, dropping her bag in the doorway, 'I know it's rude of me just to turn up, but I'm trusting it's okay. I knew you'd be vaccinated and you've got empty rooms.'

Now, we were relaxing after dinner.

Miranda said, 'There are such ridiculous beliefs around at the moment, things like Australia doesn't exist, the earth is flat, the moon landing was fake.'

'The Titanic didn't exist,' my husband said.

'Do you believe that?' Miranda asked.

My husband Ian laughed. 'Of course not. It's just one of those ridiculous beliefs you mentioned.

'That's a relief,' Miranda said. 'I thought for a minute—' and we all laughed.

After dinner Miranda sipped her wine and informed us that her son Mick believes that the top politicians in most countries are robots, although the American President is too creaky to be a robot. We laughed at that too.

She narrowed her eyes in thought. 'There's one thing though that worries me. You know how there are millions of birds around the world? Well, do you ever see dead ones?'

Ian and I glanced at each other. 'Not often,' I said.

'Hmm.' Miranda was silent a moment. Then, 'I'm starting to think that birds aren't real. You know, they've been replaced by robot lookalikes that keep track of us all. They're always around. On roofs. Trees. Power poles. Always watching. A global conspiracy of all governments would make it easy to kill off all the birds and put up robots.'

We went to bed that night, somewhat relieved that "birds aren't real" was the worst we could expect from Miranda.

But I found myself thinking. Drone technology had to come from somewhere.

318 words

A BOX OF CASH

She looked the caller up and down. He was dressed in such a strange way, tartan golf pants and a blue velvet jacket over what seemed to be a string vest singlet sort of thing. She frowned.

'Why?'

He bent to open the box he'd placed near his feet. She peered in to see stacks of money, clearly an enormous amount, and her eyes widened. She stared at him, and he said, '$10,000 of your dollars, I mean, $10,000 dollars for the name badge.'

She shook her head and he mistook the motion for a negative response. 'Do you want more?'

'Are you crazy?' she demanded. 'It's a kid's name badge that my daughter found on the beach, in the sand. It must have been there for ages. The rhinestones are mostly missing and a couple of the letters. My daughter Felicity is convinced the word on it is Fliss, a nickname for Felicity. It's not worth ten cents!'

She had to be honest about it, it really was just rubbish. But—$10,000! 'Tell me why,' she demanded, hands on hips.

'The badge is a gift for the woman who will become the first female leader of the country 27 years from now. She had it made for her swearing-in as President. Her opposition stole it and flung it back in time.

'I've travelled back to find it and today is the furthest back I can go. If I could go back another three months, I would prevent the badge being lost on the beach.

'When I return to the future, the present will change: the badge won't exist in your time any more.' He didn't say what he was thinking: *You won't remember this conversation or discover that the badge is encrusted with pink and champagne diamonds, not rhinestones.*

The mother of the future President could never explain the box of money found in the basement any more than her husband could.

323 words

THIS TIME TOMORROW

My brother Joel is a certified maths genius, a real MENSA level brain. Often such highly intelligent people are lacking in social skills—somehow the personal connections aren't so important.

I'm glad to say that Joel's not like that. He was a friendly kid. When my girlfriends and I got together, he could be entertaining and they enjoyed his company. He memorised sports statistics effortlessly. Running was his sport, and he got me into it too. Well, our parents did: he was too young to run alone.

When he was about 12 and I was 18, he told me he thought he'd cracked time travel. I laughed, of course, and he shook his head at me. 'Just the preliminary work on it,' he said, 'I haven't figured it all out.'

'Of course. You need to get that maths brain working a bit harder.'

'The thing is,' he said, 'if I do crack it in the future and I get to travel in time, then this time tomorrow I'll come here.'

'Here?' I repeated. 'The kitchen?'

'The front door. It's 3.45 now, so this time tomorrow.'

He was so confident! We told Mum and Dad when they got home and I promised to ring them if anything truly epic happened.

Joel and I waited on the front porch. I was looking over next semester's materials and Joel was doing a cryptic crossword.

We both watched the time. On the dot of a quarter to four, a car pulled up and a tall man in a suit got out. I watched open mouthed. He had gingery hair and fair skin like Joel. Bloody hell! When he got close, he said, 'Sandra?'

'Joel?'

He shook his head, smiling broadly. 'No, I'm Hugo.'

Did I say Joel enjoyed pranks and practical jokes? Hugo was doing maths at uni and knew Joel through his advanced classes.

I married Hugo a few years later. Our time travel meeting makes a good story for our kids.

329 words

VILLAGE LIFE

When we crash landed on this planet a year ago—I figure it's been about a year in human terms—I thought I was a goner but Rickson and I survived, so that was good. Then when we were rescued by the locals, I was scared stiff. They're enormous, mottled-skin people, big fang-type teeth, human shape generally speaking, but that's something they didn't do—speak. It was eerie.

Rickson and I figured out pronto that they were telepathic. They looked at us like we were insects when we talked.

We ended up in this village of huge people, just as scary as the others, but at least these villagers talk. As I've learned the language, it seems they're the untouchables of this world, deficient because they don't have telepathy. We fitted right in, talk-wise, and otherwise too. The village people are the tradesmen and women, the doers. The others are too superior to dirty their hands fixing things that go wrong.

Rickson and I are both handymen, and after trying other things we found ourselves on a painting crew. It was so boring it was killing me. There were so few colours available, so one day I hung onto some samples of the colours and combined them. Then I painted an abstract painting.

Rickson had a go and he wasn't half bad. He painted me standing in front of our little house. The villagers went wild. They'd never seen anything like either painting. Nor had the telepathic ones. I reckon imagination is something that never developed on this world, and Rickson and I have enough imagination for all of them.

We live in the lap of luxury now. Our paintings are all the rage and sell for a ton of money. A couple of our fellow villagers are trying their hand at painting and that's causing a lot of excitement. They're not as good as us.

I can still only do splashy abstracts and I've changed my name to Picasso!

330 words

SEVEN DAYS

Voices woke Clarry up. Flinging his mangy covering off, he promptly banged his head on the cave wall. Ears ringing, he lay back, listening.

The voices were young. Climbers, hikers, he didn't care as long as they didn't know he was there. The bright desert light hurt his eyes, and he turned away from the narrow entrance and reached for the last of his rum. He leaned on an elbow and finished the bottle, placing it with the other detritus of his current camp.

Clarry sniffed. He could smell salt. He shook his head. Saltwater. Like the beach. The voices above him became excited, shrill. A couple of high-pitched female voices among them for sure. Then he could hear water. Water sloshing. Back and forth kind of sloshing. Like waves. He shook his head again. Gotta give up the rum.

The sounds continued and he crawled through the cave to the entrance where the brilliant light was dimmed. Before he reached the opening he could see the water. The blue of deep water. Outside his cave among the rocks rimming the desert. His mouth hung open in disbelief and he crawled right out. The rocks outside the cave were a good two metres above the water but for all he knew the cave was gonna get swamped. He reached back for his swag, tucking the edges of the old cloth around his stuff. Slinging it over his back, he climbed up.

Wearily, he reached the top, the lake or whatever filling the air with its smells and sounds, to see young people grouped near a tour bus.

They saw him and fell silent, a couple slapping hands to their mouths in shock.

'Oh no,' the only adult with them said. Clarry didn't remember anything after that.

Ambrose, the only adult, appointed two students to dismantle the inland sea, two to organise a comfortable seat for Clarry on the bus, and two to read up on the spell, or spells, needed to convince a non-magical human that he had been dreaming.

'We'll put him back this time next week. A swaggie won't know he's missed seven days.'

356 words

GREEN FLOWERS

I feel uneasy. There's something odd, that niggling feeling of something overlooked, something missing, feathering the nape of my neck. I look around.

The office looks normal, I think. Regina has put fresh flowers in the vase on the low table to impress visitors—her idea. I look closely at them. They are really fresh. I don't remember seeing them before, these particular flowers. Well, obviously I wouldn't if she's only just put them there, but I don't recognise them at all. They are unusual, the petals green with a pale blue edging, like the frill on a little girl's dress.

I stare at them. Green flowers. Blue edging. I can't remember seeing them before. Ever.

I tap the intercom and it makes a hollow noise. I look at it. It isn't my intercom. My intercom is light yellow with black letters and digits on grey keys. This, this whatever it is, is silver. With black keys. Tiny images or letters are embossed or printed on the black keys.

Experimentally I tap the big one on the bottom. A female voice says, 'Yes boss?'

'Regina?'

'Ah, no, boss. Who's Regina?'

'It's ok,' I say hurriedly and sit back, lifting my finger from the strange device.

I'd arrived at the office a bit early to catch up. The only thing out of the ordinary was the way I'd left the elevator. Entering the lift on the ground floor I'd noticed the wet patch on the floor just inside the door but had stupidly stepped on it as I left the elevator. My feet slid out from under me and I cracked the back of my head on the floor of the elevator, the door bumping me as it tried to close. I stayed there a few moments until my head stopped spinning. Went into my office. Shut the door. Felt the back of my head. No blood.

Now, a strange voice, strange flowers. I look around. Strange office actually. I study my desk. The calendar looks wrong somehow. The date is right, Monday September 22. I open a drawer. Strange things inside.

Slowly I turn my chair to face the window. And wish I hadn't.

364 words

PAINFUL REALITY

'I'd really like to understand why no one in power changed things so the world wouldn't, you know, implode, or die. Why didn't they?'

It's hard to stay cheerful, to be positive, even with all the veggies growing so well. Knowing my boy won't ever have a wife, a partner, children—a future. I should have had the courage to … well, he's here now, and I'll try to keep him well for as long as I can.

'No matter how often you bring it up, I won't be able to explain it. I've told you, when people make money from bad things, those bad things continue. People made money from letting the earth spoil and from letting the sky fill with such pollution and poison that humans may die out.'

I pick up and empty out a half bucket of water on the row of tomato plants. The action helps to disguise my sadness—humans *will* die out—but although he reads the old books and the few newspapers I saved, he doesn't realise this yet.

'I know, you've told me, but… it's just so…'

'Incredible, yes. The oceans were warming and rising, people by the million moved from place to place, agricultural zones shifted all around the world. Where we are now—'

He shrugged. He knows this refrain. '—where we are now you could never grow carrots or potatoes before. I know. But why did the politicians—'

I feel a surge of the old anger, the useless teeth-grinding fury at those stupid, stupid people. 'They bombed each other because they could. Like a cranky child might hurt a small animal just because he can.'

My boy lifts his face to the sky, where the sun has been hidden since before his birth. Where it will stay hidden until we are all gone.

'Then the power died—' he prompts, despite knowing the story, and I nod.

'And no one could find out why because all communication stopped.' My breath catches in my throat. All those people.

'And so we grow our own veggies,' he parrots an old optimism, 'and lucky we are that we can.' He nods, happy in this final good thing to think about.

I turn my face from him to dig for a carrot. *And glad I am,'* I think, *'that you don't know what's coming.*

394 words

Frances Goodey

TRAINS AND SPACESHIPS

'You know what a train is, don't you? You've studied history?'

'I think so. But trains were on Earth, and we're not.'

'I'm sure you learned about this before the sleep. I hope being out so long hasn't damaged your memory.'

I dared a mildly scathing look at him. Couldn't be too cheeky, he'd tell my parents. He clearly remembered the old life while I was only two years old when I went into the sleep. He had lived it; I had to study and learn and memorise.

I'd learned what a train was, and it didn't make sense that our spaceship was called a train.

'Can you explain?'

Why should I? He's the teacher!

I took a deep breath and scrunched my face, trying to think. I remembered the look of a train—a leading engine (that's a word we still use in space!) pulling behind it a connected string of cars, or carriages. A train of carriages! That must be it. In the nursery, the little kids make trains of connected blocks they pull along the floor. Trains on Earth carried people. I remembered the pictures.

I explained my thinking and he agreed I was right. But how did that relate to where we were, in space, en route to a new world which we'd reach when I was an old man?

Would we have trains there? I didn't risk asking a question like that!

He took a call and said he'd be back soon. 'While I'm away,' he said, 'think about trains and spaceships. How might they be connected?'

I wandered over to the faux window and looked out on what might be there if only we could see it. The images were supposed to be a good representation of the galaxy we were travelling through.

Light from distant suns glinted off frozen worlds, sparking colours of all kinds. I wonder sometimes if colours can freeze, colours that will never melt, and if there are colours that our human eyes can't see.

A string of planetoids whizzed past (or appeared to), a big one followed by a batch of smaller ones—like a planetoid engine pulling little ones behind.

Oh! I wonder if that's why the spaceship is a train, or at least part of one. Ours could be one of many, a long string of spaceships heading out to new worlds since the old one was wrecked so thoroughly. I bet that's it.

I wonder if our spaceship is the engine, or just one of the little followers behind?

423 words

THE BOOKS

'Can you really be thinking of staying here, my lady? How would you live? How would you deal with unknown enemies?' Quincy squared his shoulders and stood tall. He had a decision to make, himself, if the lady should prefer to remain in this unfamiliar place. He eyed the two books on the desk.

Lady Leona twirled in her gorgeous gown, on her beautiful shoes, laughing to herself. 'I can choose, can I not? Here, I do not have to follow the rules laid down by others. Ha!' And she began to inspect the strange room.

Quincy sat on the wooden chair at the desk and bent to turn the empty pages of the second book, a handmade album. Only the first page was inscribed. 'My lady, there is wizardry at work. This book is waiting to be filled with spells.'

'Look!' she called. 'Can this be an image of me?' She was standing before a large formal portrait of a beautiful woman who had Leona's big brown eyes, her remarkable eyebrows, her bright titian hair. Quincy joined her to inspect the picture and he laughed.

'Yes, it is an image of you!'

'I shall not think of the book. I am here now, and I may stay.' Leona frowned. 'How am I here, *and* in the book?'

'The wizard who lives here creates spells and stories. He created you, and me, and somehow you are here in his world and somehow I am here too. Do you not feel the spell-dust in the room?'

Returning to the desk and pushing the album aside, Quincy examined the other book. 'Here we are, both of us. Look how powerful I am!'

Leona leaned against him and studied the open pages of the book of fairy tales. 'In the book, you are. In the book, I am beautiful, as here, but there I am helpless. There, I need you to guard me, but here I feel strong and brave.' Leona stared at her picture in the book, turned to the picture on the wall. 'I think the wizard may be very glad that I have escaped the book.'

A door opened further down the room and something *click, clicked* on the stone-flagged floor. There was an aged wizard leaning on his walking stick, staring at his visitors.

Quincy stood tall, keeping the book in sight. He knew spell-dust had brought them here, whether purposefully or not; there had still to be traces of it on the page and he would make a dash for it.

Lady Leona could make her own choice.

430 words

INTO THE POT

New as I was to the camp, I didn't have any trouble settling in. I'd been taught everything I needed to know, and I'd volunteered to be incarcerated.

It was because I was so young, not quite nineteen, that I'd been trained. All I had to do was show the bastards that I could cook, and I'd be in. And I was so angry at our overseers that I could be trusted to take any risk necessary. I was there to test a rumour, the one that claimed all the humans in one camp got out when they fed the aliens something that killed them all.

I was standing at the electrified wire fence gazing out at the desert, more stones than sand, more grey than sandy, when one of Them approached from behind. I knew he was there from the stench.

Why couldn't aliens have been friendly cuddly loveable creatures? Nice-looking in some way?

I gritted my teeth and turned to him. I hoped it wasn't latrine duty again. Laundry wasn't bad, sweeping the grounds was bearable, but latrine was atrocious.

'Kitchen, cook,' he gurgled at me and turned away. I presume he turned away. His back was identical to his front, metal-looking overlapping plates like little shields all I could see. Somewhere inside was a body, eyes and a mouth. I guess I'd find out if I got to serve what I'd be cooking.

The list I'd memorised occupied my thoughts as I learned what to do in the kitchen. It took me three days to find out, oh so casually, that the four items on my list were present. Now it was up to me to introduce them, one at a time, into the food our alien masters would be eating. One of the items on the list, it was hoped, would be lethal to them.

Two of us had the same list, two who would try to get on the cooking roster at two different camps. With luck, if the rumour was true, one of the four items was the answer.

Washing plates and scrubbing vegetables and cutting up meat kept me occupied while I awaited my chance. I had to do it alone—there was no way to tell which of my fellow humans might betray me for a reward.

Then, finally, allowed to stir a pot of bubbling meat unsupervised, I pulled the small almost-overripe lemon from my jacket pocket. No time like the present to get the job started. I quickly cut it in half and squeezed the juice into the pot.

That's one ticked off.

433 words

Frances Goodey

A SHORT-TERM SOLUTION

The young officer straightened his tie and pulled his shoulders back. Waiting to be called into the office, he glanced at the festive Christmas decorations. Posters displayed data about the dozens of spaceships ready to depart, with millions of frozen seeds and animal embryos, and thousands of humans.

He knew that escaping from a world now quite hostile to humans was the only possible solution. It had been for decades, during which time the spaceships had been built and the plans laid to save humanity.

No one on the spaceships would ever see the planet they were headed for, but their grandchildren's grandchildren should.

A family entered quietly and took their seats. They began talking about the posters, the little girl obviously unhappy.

'We haven't seen many other kids,' the teenage boy complained.

'Not yet maybe but they're here. You'll make friends in no time. Plus you'll have an amazing career, you know, doing things that you could never do here.'

The boy caught the officer nodding. and the officer said, 'All the adults are young too, like me.'

The dad agreed, saying, 'My wife and I will be among the oldest, and we're not old.'

His son said, 'I understand. It has to be families with kids already and couples who can have kids in the future.'

His little sister piped up, laughing, 'That's you, Timmy, you have to have children!'

'So do you,' he snapped at her.

She stared at him then turned to her mother, tearfully. 'Do I, Mum, do I have to have children? I'm only seven.'

Glaring at her son, the mother hugged her. 'You don't have to worry about that for years and years. Come on, let's go for a walk,' the mother said, taking the girl's hand. As they left, the dad turned to his son. 'I know you'll cope but we're worried about Anita. I don't think she really understands that we're leaving

Earth altogether, never seeing any family or friends again, ever, and never coming back.'

The officer looked at them thoughtfully. 'Excuse me, sir,' he said. 'I can offer you a short-term solution to help your daughter, if you like,' and he told them his idea.

When the mother and daughter returned, the young officer was talking into his phone. Quite loudly.

'Has the old man boarded yet? Our ship is really lucky to have him, for sure. What about his reindeer? Will they settle okay? Oh that's good. And you've got plenty of food for them?'

He was quiet for a moment, then said clearly, 'How many elves came with him? I hope it's enough. There's a lot of kids who'll want presents.'

The little girl's eyes were shining.

450 words

A NEW YORK EVENT

Damn! I forgot to ask Brad how much I should tip the young bloke carrying my bag to the room. As if I couldn't carry it myself but when in Rome, and all that. Plus Brad has told me to take advantage of everything on offer. My creative genius has earned it, he told me solemnly.

I'm taking everything in, ready to tell Josie back in Sydney what a brand-new top hotel in New York is like. Everything shiny bright, chandeliers galore, thick carpet underfoot, non-hotel-type paintings on the walls.

The bellboy sees me looking at them as we pass together down the long corridor. 'They're all paintings by friends of the owner,' he offers. 'Maybe one day worth a lot and for painters at the start of their careers, this is good exposure.' I think that's what he said, his accent is different from Brad's.

As we approach my door, 1745, a girl walks into the corridor from another room. Must be about 1737 or 1739, I'd say. She's in a floaty white outfit, maybe what they used to call a negligee way back when—I remember my Aunty Ellen wearing one when she visited years ago.

The girl—she must be about 18—stands in the middle of the hallway looking around. She must see us approaching but doesn't react. She lifts her hands shoulder-height as though exasperated, turns and goes back into the room.

'Someone's running late,' I comment.

The bellboy makes an odd sound and I glance at him. He looks at me with wide eyes. 'You saw her?'

'Who, the girl? Of course.' I give him a quizzical look. 'What are you talking about?'

'Do you remember which door she came out of?' he asks. I point doors two ahead. Then we're level with it. It has a sign on it. Utilities.

'Utilities?' I'm confused. 'How could she…?'

He stops to tap the lock and the door swings out into the corridor, not inward like guests' rooms. I'm standing open-mouthed. When she came out, the door didn't do this. The room is full of shelves laden with all kinds of boxes and packets. I see toilet rolls and tissue boxes and plastic buckets of soap and tiny shampoo bottles. Mops. Vacuum cleaners.

I look at the bellboy and he shrugs. 'Not everyone sees her.'

He shuts the door and we reach my room. He places my bag on a low wooden rack affair and turns to leave. I'm reaching for my wallet and he holds up a hand.

'No money, thanks, sir. But I'd appreciate it if you mention the girl at reception,' he says. 'I see her all the time but the other staff think I'm nuts.'

453 words

THE LAST NIGHT

Jack and Denny stayed in the basement between their hourly tours of inspection, which took precisely 15 minutes to complete when they moved quickly. Tonight, they were back in the basement in just under 14 minutes. That left them 46 minutes to have another drink, open another packet of crisps, demolish another chocolate biscuit or two, and have another drink.

Tonight, their basement was party headquarters. Both men were finishing up tonight. No more night shifts. No more shifts of any kind. As it happened their birthdays were within a week of each other and they were retiring. Since management of the security company and the various companies that occupied the building during the day had not deigned to farewell these honest and faithful servants with any recognition at all, they were performing their own send-off ceremony.

Half asleep at 3.47am, Denny suggested they give the next check a miss. Jack agreed. They'd go at 4.58, do the 5am check next. Missing one check after all these years, on their last night—who'd ever know, what harm could it do? Jack set his phone alarm in case they dozed off.

The two security dogs relaxed, having been gifted a big helping of their favourite dog food as part of the party activities.

The television set high on one wall was on low volume, a football match playing. It also emitted both electronic noise and warmth.

The aliens arrived on the roof and made their way in through gaps in an air conditioning unit. They all fell to the floor which was unexpectedly far below and most of them were injured. The air was thick with such moisture that three of the group passed out and had to be carried. They all knew they had to get out of the building, but their entry point was inaccessible, impossibly high above them.

Electronic signatures and warmth were everywhere, machinery emitting heat in all directions. Skirting these occasional wells of warmth and electricity, the visitors headed for huge doors, which slid open as they approached, to reveal a spacious room. To their alarm the doors shut behind them.

High above their heads was writing, lights, rows of buttons. Clearly a button had to be touched. With athletic grace, the three tallest raised others among them to the best height they could, and the topmost one extended a particularly long wand to touch the nearest button.

In the basement, the men were dozing, beer cans in hand, when the dogs abruptly stood, silently, to gaze at the elevator doors.

When the doors opened, the aliens were aghast at the sight of two fierce gigantic many-toothed creatures.

Management had to watch the security footage to figure out what happened to the security guards and their dogs.

461 words

BUILDING CHARACTER

'The manual says adversity will build character.'

'What does that mean, "build character"?'

'Adversity builds character,' M09 repeated.

'Adversity means hardship or danger, I understand that, but you and I wouldn't want to face adversity so why…' P142's voice would have sounded exasperated, if it could.

M09 and P142 gazed at the human child only just now removed from its life-support system. It lay on a specially-woven soft matting that absorbed liquid and other waste that the child's body produced.

They had needed an extra section of soft matting to place over the child as it regularly sprayed liquid waste upward, in a gravity-defying manner that was, simply put, not only unexpected but disconcerting.

This human child was the first of the more than 5000 such individuals to be raised to maturity by M09 and P142. Other mechanicals would be brought into service as the numbers rose.

'This baby must have a strong mind, well-formed and independent. It must have a strong, resilient body. It must develop attitudes to life that will make it … strong and resilient.'

'But it's cruel, and callous. You and I wouldn't like to have mean things done to us.' P142's nursing and nannying chip, recently activated for the first time, had a high level of empathy.

M09's head wobbled in the robotic equivalent of a shrug, which also passed for a sigh. 'It's our job to make this young human …'

'I know, I know, strong and resilient, with character. But what does it mean, character, what does character mean?'

An instant's reflection allowed M09 to say, '"The mental and moral qualities distinctive to an individual".'

'But this human is only a baby. It has yet to develop any qualities at all.'

'Right! And from the beginning we need to train it to develop … strength and resilience. It's in the manual. They will help it survive, and thrive, when we reach the planet.'

'Well, I think,' said P142, 'that if we try to give it what its human parents would, care and love and sustenance, it will develop strength and resilience as it grows.'

'Of course, we will care for it and nourish it but with the constant aim of giving it strength and resilience.'

P142 it sighed its own robotic sigh. 'All right, let's get on. What do you plan for it?'

'It's about to face its first adverse event. You and I don't exactly look like human parents, do we? Overcoming a natural revulsion at the sight of us will be the first step.'

The baby stirred and turned over. It looked up at the metallic faces with no eyes and no nose and no mouth, and it gurgled. And waved its chubby fingers. And reached for them with a gummy giggle that strangely disturbed M09 even as it charmed P142.

470 words

ELECTRONIC JUNK

'Give it to me! I found it!'

Rosalie sighed. 'For goodness' sake, you two. I can't wait for you to grow up.'

Moana evaded her brother's reach and showed her mother a small black gadget. 'I found this in the box from the ceiling—'

'You did not!'

Rosalie said, 'It's old so go and see Grandad. Go together. Calmly.'

Their grandad Conor would never have known they'd been fighting, so sweet was their demeanour as he examined the device.

'I know I've seen one before but I'm not sure. Mum would know. It's more her era than mine.'

'Greatgran? Are you sure?'

Greatgran Lisa, now 93, was fairly sprightly. She was one of a huge group in society, the long-surviving elderly, and she lived an energetic life with many friends. She had an apartment to herself at the back of the family home where the youngsters were always welcome.

'This,' she pronounced, 'needs a battery. Or two. Little tiny triple As.'

'But what is it?'

'It's a camera. It holds hundreds, maybe thousands, of photos. Where did you find it?'

'In that box of stuff Dad found in the ceiling. You remember a few weeks ago, boxes of stuff left by people who lived here before. Even an old Christmas tree. Dad cleaned it up and it's…'

'I know, I know. I'm old, not stupid. I saw it in the living room.'

The kids wilted. Greatgran sighed. 'Sorry, sorry. I'm feeling the bones in my bum today.' She looked at them. 'They are 93, you know. What are you giggling about?'

She continued, 'It's 2068, right?' The pair nodded. 'Christmas Eve?' She grinned at them and Jacob pulled a face. 'And this camera has to be from the early 20 hundreds, even the late 1900s—'

'So long ago,' Moana whispered.

'—so you need the kind of batteries that might be among the detritus of the splendid technological past we so enjoyed. Ask your dad about the box of electronic junk in the garage rafters. You never know.'

She pushed the camera back at them and struggled to her feet. 'I'm being picked up for Canasta in five minutes. I've got to get ready. Go.'

Their dad was amazed to find an unopened packet of four tiny batteries marked AAA in the box of ancient relics. But it was their grandad they asked to open the neat little compartment for the batteries.

'You turn it on,' Moana told him.

The black panel on the face of the camera lit up. More than 20 tiny images appeared, faces, sunsets, a stage, many more faces. Jacob was about to touch one when the camera expired.

'It was gone in a flash,' Jacob later told Greatgran Lisa. 'But you could say we caught a glimpse of how you used to live.'

470 words

NO TEETH, NO CLAWS

'In the olden days, on old Earth,' Milton began, and paused. 'Have I told you this one before?'

'Da-ad!' both boys exclaimed. 'You start all your stories like that.' They pulled faces at each other and turned back to their father.

'Well, that's where the stories were, on old Earth.'

'We know, go on, tell us,' Ryder urged. 'Tell the one about the little animal covered in soft fur that was so cute you could cuddle it and it's breathing would rumble when it was happy.'

His dad laughed. 'I think you've told us that one now yourself.'

Oliver leaned across from his bed. 'Ryder forgot to say that the furry animal had sharp teeth and claws. What was it, Dad?'

'A cat. It had lots of big cousins in many countries—lions, tigers, panthers, man-eaters all if they could catch one of us. Some of them were bigger than me.'

Ryder shivered. 'Did other animals have sharp teeth and claws, Dad?'

‘Yes, of course. To defend themselves with and to eat with.’

‘But we don’t, do we, Dad? We don’t have sharp teeth and claws.’

Oliver leaned over to his brother, opening his mouth wide. ‘Course we don’t silly.’ They investigated each other’s mouths. No teeth at all.

They looked at the ends of their fingers. No claws. Nothing. Just rounded nubs of flesh.

‘Is it true, Dad, what the boys at school say, that we should have teeth and claws? That we do have them but they get taken out when we’re babies?’

‘Yes, I’m afraid it is true. We’re born with claws on our fingers and as we grow, teeth grow too, but we have treatment that stops more from coming.’

‘But why, Dad, why can’t we have what grows in us naturally?’

Oliver, older by a couple of years, had been through this already. He looked at his dad, who nodded for him to go ahead.

‘If we had teeth and claws, we might hurt our owners. And they love us and don’t want us to be punished for hurting them with teeth and claws that we can’t help growing. So they stop them from growing.’

Milton knew already that Oliver was going to be the troubled one. The boy’s voice was defiant. ‘Why do we have to belong to those giants, anyway, it’s not fair.’

Milton looked gloomily at his sons. ‘We chose to come to their planet, boys. We’re lucky they think we’re cute and interesting. We might be pets to them but at least we’re alive.’

After tucking the boys in for the night, Milton paused to gaze at them. He shook his head. The time was approaching fast. He’d have to prepare them for the future. He pondered his own brief encounters in the breeding rooms, years ago now. He’d have to tell them about females.

474 words

PURPLE PYRAMIDS

'I want you to try for lucid dreaming tonight, Nancy,' Dr Fengold said. She fixed me with her dark brown eyes and willed me to listen to her.

'Don't stare at me like that,' I said, shaking my shoulders and turning aside. 'It makes me nervous when anyone stares at me.'

'I know,' she said, 'but I'm serious and I want you to listen to me. Look at me.'

Sighing, I took my eyes from the exotic Egyptian scene in its beautiful golden frame on the wall and looked at her. One glance back to the tiny figure off to one side lounging on a flying carpet with a purple pyramid in the background and I was all hers. I wish I could see that little man a lot closer, a lot bigger. It was a man; I could make out a bare chest …. I concentrated on the doctor.

'Now,' Dr Fengold began, 'I'll reiterate. You are an adult woman with no close friends. No romantic partner. No siblings. No extended family. You claim this situation doesn't bother you ….'

I put in, 'Would it help you to be reminded that an abusive childhood in an extended family'—my fingers put air quotes around "extended family"—'all the older ones abusing the younger ones, is the very reason I lead a solitary life quite happily?'

'Nancy, I know all that. And I know that if you keep on having the awful nightmarish dreams you have, you won't be able to make a fresh start at all.'

I looked at her. 'Hence the lucid dreaming?'

'Tell yourself as you settle for sleep what you will see in your dreams. Make it something you don't normally see, something interesting, or exciting—oh, a green elephant, a miniature tiger on a leash, a prince inviting you to a ball, anything.'

I glanced at the framed Egyptian picture on the wall and said quietly, 'Purple pyramids maybe.'

'Perfect,' she said.

My dream began in the usual way. I was on the top step of a set of steps outside a huge church. The one my extended family attended. Usually I was surrounded by family members who ushered me inside, but this time, with 'purple pyramids' echoing in my mind, I slipped through the crowd off to one side. I turned my back to the church and gazed into the distance.

There were no buses or cars or houses lined up side by side, with doors shut and curtains drawn. There was a disturbance in the golden air in the distance and the sky tore open with a rippling sound. I stared, thinking, 'purple pyramids, purple pyramids', and the tiny figure on the flying carpet swept through the opening in the sky. It came closer and closer and grew bigger and bigger. I stepped back to make room on the landing.

477 words

A MEMORY

The old man turned 90 yesterday. That meant he was born in 2005. 90 long years ago. The children, well, some of them, were interested to meet him, with his craggy wrinkled face and dark-spotted hands.

One of the little girls, Emily, quite liked his hands; they were like her granny's even though granny wasn't as old as this old man. Emily was the only one to approach him. He put out his hand to shake hers and she was quite relaxed about doing it. That's when Emily noticed how his hands were like her granny's.

Her granny, who was (Emily thought) about 60 or 70, was definitely not as old as this old man. She stayed close to him, enjoying his old-man smell because it reminded her of her granny's dad. She had a vague memory of meeting him once when she was really little, probably not even at school yet. He died.

This old man, whose name was Conor, was visiting the school today. The teachers often had visitors who were old because most of the children rarely saw old people. The school also had regular visits from mums who brought their babies to school for the children to look at, and touch, and sometimes hold. There weren't many babies around, and not many old people either.

Emily's mum, who was the daughter of Emily's granny, said that there were actually a lot of old people but they didn't live near the young people; most of them lived in nice villages where they had lots of friends and activities to do, while the young people, like Emily's mum and dad, got to live in the houses that the old people used to live in.

Emily's mum was expecting a baby in two more months, and that meant the government would let Emily and her family live in a much nicer house, and her dad would have a better job.

Emily's mum and dad talked to Emily in a way that most mums and dads didn't talk to their children. Emily understood that when the sea levels rose and seawater covered the outside edges of the country, people moved. Lots of houses got washed away or were now standing in the sea.

Old people were encouraged to leave their homes and young people with babies got the best places. Many people also came from islands that the sea swallowed up. That was another reason old people got moved into villages, so the island people would have homes. Lots of the island people had babies, so that was good. Good for the country, Emily's mum and dad said.

The old man, Conor, leaned over to Emily and said, 'I remember being your age.'

Holding the old man's hand while he listened to some of her classmates singing to him, Emily had the idle thought, 'I wonder what I'll remember when I'm 90.'

482 words

STORIES WITH WORD COUNT 485-871

ONE LAST JOB

Thompson wished, not for the first time, that he had a flair for languages. Dealing with foreigners would be so much easier if he could converse with them. Nothing too formal, just have a conversation.

He envied Rossini who spoke three besides her native Italian, and now she was learning a fifth from the little fellas they'd picked up on that last planet.

That had been a good break. Good weather, strange but tasty food, amazing scenery (he'd like to bring his wife and kids to holiday there some time), while the locals, alien as heck, were attractive little guys, furry and colourful, with big eyes and a helpful nature. It was tempting to pile on the work since they were so willing. Now they were standing with Rossini near the ladder down to the pale sandy ground.

One was named Bolo, who was mostly green, and the other was the pink and purple one whose name Thompson couldn't remember.

'Rossini,' he called, 'what are they saying to you now?'

'I think I'm getting the gist of it. Bolo,' *the green one*, thought Thompson, 'says his people are great travellers. Every space craft that visits their planet leaves with two or three of his people.'

Rossini and Bolo came back in and Rossini said as she passed him, 'Vilog'll be back in a minute. He has one last job.'

Thompson nodded distractedly. He had the feeling something hadn't been done. Had he checked that last lot of samples? He had. He knew he had. They were all stowed away, neatly, hygienically. He was satisfied with the collection of soils and vegetation, and signs of animal life. They hadn't seen any, but there was scat enough to show they existed. That was for the scientists back home and for whoever landed here next.

What hadn't been done? The water supply was good. The food supplies more than adequate. He knew there was something. They'd be taking off soon, once pink-and-purple came back inside, pulled up the ladder. He'd probably remember once they were under way.

He could see the alien bobbing along, holding a long stick high above him. A metallic gleam catching Thompson's eye made him realise it was a pole, a metal pole.

Peering through the viewer above the computer at his fingertips, Thompson asked Rossini, 'What's he doing?'

'They like to place a marker whenever they go to a new planet. They record it and send messages and pictures back to their people.'

'Huh.' Thompson's grunt was contemplative. Now he remembered the job not done.

'Hey, Rossini, did you plant a flag for us, you know, claiming this empty potentially valuable planet for all humanity?'

She stared at him. Looked out at the little alien. Looked back at him. They watched the alien flag open up in the gentle breeze of whatever this planet would be called, and not in any Earth language.

485 words

IN THE ATTIC

Henry could never bring himself to tell anyone the truth about what happened to Marisa Sanchez, about how he watched her disappear and was too cowardly to follow her. He just went home and never told anyone. Not that anyone would believe him.

He was tempted: when the teachers talked to the class about stranger danger, when groups of girls burst into tears, when the funeral service was on.

He even wrote down exactly what happened, minute by minute, but he tucked it away in the back of a drawer. He knew no one would believe him; he hardly believed it himself.

He and Marisa had been to Tommy Sharpe's 12th birthday party. All the class was there, and a bunch of parents. They'd had fun—Marisa had won a prize for pinning the tail on the donkey. Henry ate too much of the festive food and knew the walk to Marisa's would be good for him. He wasn't due home until 5 o'clock, so he accepted Marisa's suggestion that they explore the attic of her house. She'd always wanted to do it, she told him, but not alone. It was creepy, she told him. Having a boy along would be good, she told him.

Her dad was home, watching football. He just waved them away when Marisa said they were going to the attic. He didn't even look at them.

The attic was full of old junk. An old trunk covered with travel stickers—where was Azerbaijan? he'd wondered—and baby clothes and a cot and old clothes hanging on racks. A dusty chest of drawers with stuff spilling out. Then there was the picture frame. An enormous golden frame that a man could walk through. It seemed to be freestanding, nothing whatever supporting it, about a metre out from a wall. It was strange. He pushed it and it was rock solid. They walked in circles around it, puzzled.

Marisa's family had only been in the house a few months. She wasn't sure her parents had ever been up in the attic. Her mum had said once it had a bad feeling to it, one of the reasons Marisa wanted company.

Finally, Henry had said, 'I'm gonna go through it,' even though he was scared. He didn't know why, he just was. But when Marisa said, 'Ladies first, if you please' and hip-bumped him out of the way, he was secretly relieved and gestured her to go ahead.

He couldn't believe it when she vanished as her whole body entered the frame. His face froze. He shook his head and, bravely he felt, put his head into the frame. The wall was in front of him, with old pictures and dusty feathery decorations and peeling wallpaper. He walked around the frame and came back to the front of it. He actually lifted a foot to walk through, but he couldn't do it. Marisa's dad was still watching footy when Henry went home.

494 words

FLOWERS

The three elderly men settled back into their seats as the jet slowed over the widespread jungle. Twins Jed and Noah and their old mate Sam were enjoying this unique opportunity to contribute.

They had cleared the tops of the mountain range, which had lakes of what looked like water here and there in hidden nooks at high levels. They had noted the geographical location of each lake and already their people in the spaceships beyond the clouds would be preparing robotic drones to swoop down to take samples of the liquids in the lakes.

They knew if anything went wrong and they didn't survive this survey of the new world, the would-be settlers in the spaceships would be sad but in the long run, as part of the collective, they themselves would be no great loss. In a new colony they could father children but were too old to raise them. What would be missed were their talents, their skills, their accumulated knowledge.

They were feeling very optimistic, sending regular reports back upstairs. Green trees, what seemed to be grasses, both short and high shrubbery. In the distance were glints of the one large body of water they planned to land near.

Noah thought he saw a trail in one area of long grass. If he was right, that meant animals. All the signs were there for optimism: a new world for a new people, long-exiled from Mother Earth. An empty new world as far as sentient beings went, for nowhere had there been evidence of unnatural structures such as dwellings or dams or fences.

Sam assumed manual control of the jet, preparing it to slow enough to hover before settling on the patch of soil they'd already chosen to land on. The twins, peering through windows at each side, were verbally recording reports of everything they could see, their words being transmitted to the hopeful population high above.

Noah exclaimed, 'Look, flowers!' and Jed slid across the seat to join him. Sam, at the controls, called back, 'What did you see?'

and Noah replied, 'A field of colourful flowers. There's another coming up.'

Jed said quietly, 'Oh hell no. This will change everything.'

'Three minutes to landing,' Sam told them, adding, 'What, Jed?'

'They're artificial, the flowers. They're not real.'

'What are you talking about, how can you tell?'

Noah said, 'This does change everything. Jed's colour blind, he can't see what we see. We can't see what he sees. It's one of the reasons he's here.'

Jed said, 'It's usually the greens and browns in camouflage that I can pick out as unnatural; something about these flowers strikes me the same way.'

'They're panicking upstairs. I'm going to delay landing while they talk about it. How sure are you, Jed?

'One hundred percent. They're definitely artificial. Don't know what it means, but they're not natural.'

'I trust Jed's instinct,' his brother put in as Sam took them higher. He called over his shoulder to the twins, 'Upstairs are leaving it to us whether we land. What's the verdict?'

511 words

50 YEARS ON

'Oh, Mr Jimson!' The young woman's name tag said Jessica, so he smiled, 'Hi, Jessica. Call me Adam.'

'I don't think you'll need a name tag,' she said, 'but there is one for you.' She handed it to him. 'I don't think there's ever been anyone as famous as you in this old hall.'

Adam looked around. He could see lights and movement and hear music through the partially open door into the old assembly hall. He took a deep breath, ready to face them all when Jessica said, 'I work in school admin and I volunteered to be here tonight. I want to hear your speech.''

He could sense the sympathy in her voice and took the opportunity to ask, 'If you're free later on,' and she broke in, 'I'll take *you* for a drink.'

Rising, she said, 'You're the last arrival, I'll come in with you.'

He appreciated the offer of support more than she could know. No parents, no siblings, no close relatives—it's one reason he was chosen to go.

He didn't recognise anyone in the crowd. Five years ago they'd all been 28. Those who were left were now 78. They came up to him, wanting to touch him, seeing if he remembered this and that. His school friends were haggard, faces deeply lined, eyes reduced to peering out of sunken pouches. He hid his distress, deeply pleased that Jessica stayed with him the whole time.

At his own request, Adam's speech was first. He didn't want to keep people in their late 70s, his former schoolmates, up too late. Did such elderly folk go in for dinner and dancing? He'd find out.

'I've found there are only a few things people really want to know,' he began, 'so I'll be brief. Was the trip worth it? You bet! I brought back enough information to keep generations of scientists busy.

'When I left, we were all aged about 28. It took, as you know, just over 50 years to get there and back, but for me on the ship it was a journey of a little under five years.

'My destination was 25 light-years away and the journey was at almost the speed of light. I had enough supplies to last ten years, longer than the expected duration, because I couldn't re-supply anywhere!'

He said this with a chuckle—where would he find human food way out there, indeed!—but there was no reaction.

'My ship's nuclear power was fantastic. The thing about interstellar travel is it takes no energy for the spaceship to go at a constant speed. When rockets leave Earth, they only need rocket power to change speed or direction; the rest of the time they just coast.

‘I was lucky there was no serious collision with interstellar debris and as for radiation, well, I will be affected quite badly but hopefully not for another 50 years or so.’

That raised a murmur, and he flushed. The audience knew where they would be in another 50 years!

Jessica’s glance was sympathetic. Enough, he thought. Time for that drink.

516 words

OUT OF THE BOX

‘Dad, what’s this old box?’ Peter was rummaging in an old cabinet that his dad hadn’t got around to restoring. ‘It’s got a good lid,’ he said, lifting the lid a fraction and letting it drop. He placed the small dusty box on the bench beside his father’s current project.

Russell glanced at it, watching his son lift the neatly-hinged lid, exposing its inner space.

‘It’s got little toys inside,’ Peter said, ‘all colours.’ He tilted the box so his father could see them.

Russell peered into the box, his hands resting on the chair leg he’d only just removed from the wood lathe.

‘They’re cars,’ he said. ‘Your grandad collected them when he was a boy. He made the box too. I told you working with wood runs in the family.’

‘I know, I know.’

‘Go and get some rags, a damp one and a dry one, give the cars a rub down.’

A few minutes later Peter had eight cars lined up on the work bench. Two each of blue, red and yellow, one green and one black, different shapes, all about six centimetres long.

Russell watched Peter with the toys, amused to see that with the cars now smooth and shining Peter was unconsciously using the rags on the box. Turning it in all directions, gently brushing the collected dust and dirt of years off the dry brown surface. ‘There’s a letter cut into the lid,’ he said. ‘It’s a W. Or an M.’

‘Your grandad’s name was Walter.’

Peter put it aside and picked up a red car. With a finger he opened the tiny door and peered in. ‘Dad, are you sure these are cars? This one’s got a wheel inside, at the front.’ He looked inside another car. ‘This one’s got a wheel too.’

‘All cars had them once.’

‘What’s it for?’

‘Well, once, cars had to be driven. By a driver. All those cars have a wheel. It’s the steering wheel, for making the car go where the driver needed it to go.’

Peter stared at his father. ‘Really? You didn’t just get in and tell it where to take you?’

‘No. I used to see these sorts of cars when I was a little kid, but the modern cars became so safe the old ones gradually died out.’

‘Hmf.’

A memory arose in Russell’s mind. Sitting in the back seat of a fast-driven car, half thrilled and half frightened. He knew there was a darker echo there, something about a crash, and blood, and tears. He must have been very small. He shuddered the impression away.

He looked at the tiny cars, and the box. ‘Peter,’ he said, without much hope of intriguing the boy, ‘if you stripped that box thoroughly, and applied a couple of coats of varnish, it could be really beautiful again.’

‘I could! And then I could learn to make one too, couldn’t I, Dad? I could put P for Peter on the top, just like your dad did.’ He looked thoughtful, his brow furrowed. ‘I could make one as a present, couldn’t I?’

At last, Russell thought, *at long, long last, the woodworking gene has popped up*.

530 words

Frances Goodey

THE BOOKMARK

Virginia glanced up at the ceiling, hearing her daughter's feet thumping across the attic. She smiled to herself. She remembered being sent up there to explore when she'd been a child herself. There were so many interesting old things to examine.

She wondered if Rosie would find the trunk filled with old clothes. How she'd loved dressing up in long gowns and feather boas. Her school mates had too. They were so envious of the freedom she had to wander around in the old house with its many rooms. And now she was its owner, and owner of the old trunk and all the other detritus of her family's history.

It was so sad that Rosie had no companions to have such fun with.

If Rosie didn't come down soon, she just might go and join her. It might be fun to have dinner in old fashioned outfits. It might be fun to confound the staff.

Better check the progress of dinner, she thought. 'Report dinner progress.'

Cook robot turned to face her. It always annoyed Virginia when it did that. As if it needed to face her to see her when it had 360-degree vision. It seemed petty to complain, though, when she was lucky to have one at all. Doubly lucky, of course, having Rosie, since it was simply having a child at all that brought rewards, like Cook robot and the other robotic electronic staff. Concentrate, woman, she told herself.

'Repeat dinner progress.' She concentrated. Dinner was within 15 minutes of readiness.

Here was Rosie, plodding down the old wooden stairs. 'Mum, help,' she called, and Virginia hurried to her.

She held a cardboard box close to her chest. The box was softened and yellowed with age and for a moment Virginia didn't recognise it. Her face lit with joy when she did, and she exclaimed, 'The books!'

'Yes,' Rosie replied, dumping the box on the floor at the foot of the stairs. '20 of them. I counted.'

‘I remember them,’ her mother said. ‘I read all of them when I was a girl like you.’

‘It’s pretty hard to do.’ Rosie didn’t appear optimistic. ‘You have to turn every single page, and you can’t put a finger on a word and find its meaning, or go to a particular page quickly. I tried.’

‘They’re books. Real books. They were around for thousands of years before electronic ones.’

‘I know that,’ Rosie replied. ‘It’s just, you know, hard work.’ She dug into the box down one side. ‘And there’s these. Do you know what they are?’

She held a fistful of bookmarks. Yellowed, like the box, but colourful all the same. Most of them stiff card, some plastic, with holes at one end and fading tassels hanging from them.

Virginia explained, placing one inside a book. ‘Are there any more? Is there one there in the shape of a heart?’ Virginia felt herself growing younger by the moment. The heart-shaped bookmark! She would love to feel it in her hand again, to be again the 16-year-old who received it, to remember more vividly the young man she loved so madly—for a few months.

Alas, no heart-shaped bookmark.

And Cook robot was getting agitated, unhappy trying to cope with humans who ignored dinner, which had reached its maximum readiness.

552 words

THE SLEEPER SHIP

Persistent chiming inside his closed bed woke the captain gently. By the time he recovered from his long sleep and found his feet, so to speak, two full hours had passed. One doesn’t recover from years of hibernation in a hurry.

He checked his crew; none of them had been woken and all their beds were operating properly. All six of them appeared healthy when he peered in at them through the transparent lids of the beds where they floated serenely.

After a small meal, he went to the rec room where he forced himself to exercise for an hour, drinking copious amounts of water throughout. The human body suffered extreme bone loss while existing in zero gravity and this would be the first of many exercise sessions as he tried to undo the damage caused by weightlessness—and years of inactivity.

It was only when he arrived on the bridge that the officer on watch told him why he'd been woken so early. The so-called officer on watch was the system itself, known only as System. If the crew had stayed awake much longer, there would have been some effort made to give it a name, but *System* it was.

The captain hovered and drifted here and there, checking the mechanics, the electronics and the processes that kept the ship headed in the right direction, and kept safe and healthy the human crew and the thousands of hibernating people in the deep hold; the thousands of people who would settle the small world that had been chosen for them. Frozen embryos made up the rest of the human population aboard.

The captain heated a meal and began eating it while System talked to him.

It had woken him because a message had been received and a visitor was expected. The captain stopped eating and looked at the nearest screen. 'System,' he said, 'have you regularly undertaken self-checks?'

System said, 'I would chuckle if I could, Captain. I assure you I am not crazy.'

'So,' the captain resumed eating and talked around his mouthfuls, 'we've been asleep some 30 odd years and on Earth …?' He answered his own question. 'And on Earth very many years have passed.'

'Yes.' System said. 'And faster than light techniques are now in use, and a single shuttle with one man has been dropped off nearby by a ship that will land before we arrive. That's your visitor, who's coming to help you wake everyone and get you all up to speed—pardon the pun, Captain—on what's ahead.'

The captain gazed into his reconstituted coffee. 'They'll be there before us?'

'Long before.' Then, 'Your visitor is approaching, Captain.' System went on to tell the captain exactly who the visitor was, who it was that had volunteered for this job.

Floating down the corridor to the nearest washroom to freshen up, to clean his teeth, and straighten his clothes, the captain hoped to learn that the problem of artificial gravity in spaceships had been solved. Zero gravity was fun for five minutes, but the resulting physical problems were a lifelong worry. He was only 44 but his bones ached, and fluid retention made him fat.

Too late to shave. He brushed his beard and his hair. He wanted to look his best for the newcomer, his brother's great-grandson.

554 words

UGG BOOTS IN SUMMER

'He wants to see the boss,' my secretary Abigail said, waggling her eyebrows at me like an old-time comic. She turned to look back into the outer office, then back at me. 'I say "he", but, well, you know—'

'Send him in. And control those eyebrows.' She disappeared from the doorway and a little man took her place. He peeked around the door and his skinny little body followed his large, oddly shaped head into the room.

I knew what he was, so I wasn't too startled by his appearance. He was wearing close-fitting jeans that would probably fit a 12-year-old, and furry boots and a woolly coat, probably rabbit, and he was rubbing his hands to warm them up.

I was in my summer uniform and the air conditioning was going full bore. I glanced out the window. Brisbane in the summer meant people in short sleeves and light pants, and floaty cool dresses. The lucky ones, and tourists, were in shorts and singlets. But here was my visitor in his winter gear. I knew what he was all right.

He took a seat opposite me and said in a guttural voice, 'Are you the boss?'

I nodded. 'Superintendent Brownlie. And you are?'

He wriggled his backside on the chair and wrapped his arms around himself. He was obviously cold. 'You can call me Maximus.'

I smiled to myself. A big name for a little bloke. They usually chose odd names. It was thought they picked them out of books. Which reminded me—I opened a drawer and pulled out the attendance book. Abigail had been at me time and again to catch up the roster for the station.

Maximus coughed, and I glanced at him. 'Well, what can I do for you?' I knew from past encounters that he would procrastinate and delay and muck about before getting to the point, if there was one, so I opened the attendance book and picked up a pen. 'Please excuse me while I make a couple of notes'—he didn't need to know I wasn't writing about him—'and tell me how I can help.'

I glanced at him again and I saw he was taking off the fur coat. Not another one, not again. Why me? It's not fair. But as my dad used to say, fair is where you find fairy floss. I turned back to the book and said loudly, 'You'd better be fully dressed when I look at you again—I'll give you one minute—'

His gravelly voice made an unusually high-pitched sound but I didn't look up from the book. I ignored it as it continued. Had Henderson had two days off last week, or three? I made a note to ask Abigail.

The minute must be up and I couldn't stand the awful noise Maximus was making.

Oops! He couldn't manage the zipper in those tight jeans. The façade of a human body was crumpled around him—they should get better sized heads—and his tendril-covered head and upper body were bare. His lower half though, was in a bad way. That zipper had little tendrils coming out where nothing should come out. My body shrank in sympathy and I looked away.

'Abigail,' I yelled. 'Abigail!' She had two little boys. She'd know what to do.

554 words

LESS THAN 1%

July 1 Monday Last night, I received my DNA results from Ancestry.com. No surprises, especially that I'm almost 100% Celt. All four of my grandparents were of Irish descent, from both north and south, so I'm happy with that.

The report said Ireland, Scotland, Wales 88%; Great Britain 8%; Finland/NW Russia only 2%; and both Europe West and Scandinavia a measly < 1%. Less than 1%!

I've discovered through family research that I have third and fourth cousins in Finland. It's pleasant having that confirmed because I like Finland. I'll track them down and have someone to visit next time I'm there.

Four of my first cousins are doing the DNA check too, so I'll be in touch with them.

#

July 4 Thursday I've just heard from my cousin Jerry. He's a double first cousin—his mum and mine are sisters, and our fathers are brothers. Apparently, there's some deviation from my figures but his percentages are almost identical to mine. For some reason he's intrigued by the 'less than' in the <1% listing for Europe West and Scandinavia. He's going to investigate it.

There are websites and companies that delve deeper into those percentages, Jerry says. GEDmatch is the only one I've come across, but I don't think I'll bother with any more research. I'll leave it to Jerry. I don't really mind about the unknown 'less than'.

#

August 8 Thursday It's over a month and Jerry just phoned. He sounded scared. I've never heard that quiver in his voice before. He asked if I knew anything about a family connection with the Copts. I thought he said 'cops' and he had to spell it for me. I vaguely know the word. *Copts*. I've looked them up: *The Copts are an ethnoreligious group indigenous to North Africa who primarily inhabit the area of modern Egypt.*

Historically, they spoke the Coptic language, a direct descendant of the Demotic Egyptian that was spoken in late antiquity. I didn't know of any connection with the Copts, or Egyptians. Would Egypt count as Europe West, I wonder.

#

August 9 Friday Jerry just left. He came in person because he's had a visit from two Men in Black. I laughed. 'Like in the movie?' I asked, and he said, 'Exactly like in the movie.'

Apparently it's no laughing matter. He had a phone call last night, some guy told him to back off his family research. The man told him, 'Less than 1% of anything is too microscopic to worry about, don't you think?' Jerry said the man sounded intimidating and threatening.

'What did you say?' I asked him.

'I told him I was both astounded and offended.' Jerry talks like that.

'And?'

'He asked me if I'd found anything unusual in my DNA and I said, because I was bloody annoyed, "I've found some ancient information that interests me greatly", I meant the Copt Egyptian connection, and he said, "Well, alien DNA has got us this far, don't bugger things up by publicising it. Stop now that you've found it. Or else." Then he hung up.'

'Say again? What kind of DNA?'

'You heard me. "Alien DNA". In that "less than". And this afternoon these two men turned up and threatened me a bit more. Official secrets and security and prison. Leave the DNA alone.'

Jerry's just left and I'm wondering if a little bit of my DNA matches his. A tiny <1%.

561 words

THE TROUBLE WITH VODKA

Hetty turned her back on Gus who responded by walking over her to settle on the pillow, his face directly in front of Hetty's. She pretended to be asleep but was conscious of the odd breathing of her elderly pet. Gus knew perfectly well that if she wasn't up early, she was staying in bed. Today was Sunday. Sunday morning was late in bed morning, with the usual Saturday night headache.

She opened one eye just a smidgen and Gus focused instantly on that eye. She closed it immediately but Gus growled, 'Too late. I know you're awake.'

Hetty froze. Then relaxed. *What a great dream! Gus could talk!* She smiled, her eyes still closed, and said, 'Gussy, Gussy, talk some more.'

'Don't call me by that ridiculous name. I'm Augustus. Say it!' and Gus headbutted Hetty's forehead.

'Wow, that felt real,' she muttered, pulling a hand out from the blanket to rub her forehead. Her fingers brushed Gus, who batted her hand away. With the lightest touch of claws.

Hetty opened both eyes and stared at Gus. Who stared right back and said, 'What's my name?'

'Gus. I mean Augustus,' Hetty murmured obediently, her brain dancing frantically. *I'm going nuts*, she told herself, all the while staring at Gus. Augustus. 'Are you really talking to me?'

Could a cat curl its lip? Could a cat sneer?' Undoubtedly. This one was doing just that.

'I woke up this morning with a foul headache,' Gus spat at her, 'and it's your fault!'

But now Hetty had pulled herself up to a sitting position. Shaking her head in confusion, regretting it at once, she lifted Gus to settle on her lap, facing her. Hesitantly she stroked his back, massaged his arthritic shoulders.

'Rub between my ears!'

Whoa, so bossy! Hetty hastened to obey then took advantage of the purring that followed to say, 'Why is it my fault?'

I'm talking to my cat. My cat's talking to me. Who would ever believe me? I can never tell anyone.

Gus shook his head, dislodging her hand, and stood up straight. She could feel his claws through the blanket and sheet as he balanced. 'What did you put in my water bowl last night?

His claws were talons, digging. She winced and clutched her hands together to stop herself touching him. He might actually hurt her.

'What? Water! I always put water in it.'

'Not from the long bottle you drink from. You gave me your drink. It was horrible but I had to drink it. I couldn't even get water from the big white bowl in the little room. You shut the door!'

How could a cat sound so accusing? I'm considering the tone of voice my cat uses!

Hey, he drank from the toilet? I kiss that cute face sometimes! Yu-uk!

Wait! She'd given him vodka? Aah, that explained the second bottle she'd opened last night. She'd thought she'd emptied the first, but she didn't. Hooray! She didn't drink as much as she'd thought.

Gus scratched at her arm, leaving a train of red pinpricks on her skin. 'Ow!' she squealed.

'Never again,' he warned. She found herself nodding. Then shaking her head. 'No more bad water from the bottle.'

'Yes, Gu-Augustus.'

He returned to the pillow as she lay down, his rump in her face. He turned his head to add, 'That's all.'

She patted his back and reached over to rub between his ears. He purred.

Hetty never knew if it was a dream (though she did have a thin line of scabs for a few days) but from then on, Gus only purred, or growled, or hissed. No more talking.

But rubbing between his ears always made him purr.

620 words

MENTAL NOTES TO SELF

UNFAMILIAR INSECTS FRIGHTEN FARMERS

That's a good heading. Alliteration always acceptable. Ha! Wonder if Ed would go with it. It's pretty good. Mysterious. Even an agricultural paper needs mystery now and then.

> A barn in Evansdale was recently occupied by a horde of previously unknown flying insects.
>
> Said by witnesses to be huge, the insects frightened owners Fred and Marjorie Jones who said they had never seen them before.
>
> The couple, third generation owners of the farm, said one of the worst things was the extremely pungent …

Mental note to self—remember recent advice from Ed —don't use witness descriptions like sweet and pungent. Much too arty. Even tho recent subject matter concerned spill of honey in stinky warehouse.

> … extremely bitter smell that spilled out of the barn when the doors were opened.
>
> The barn had been empty for six weeks awaiting arrival of new farm equipment. The owners could not say how long the insects had occupied their barn.
>
> No picture of the insects was available.
>
> Mrs Jones shivered when describing the insects. 'They were horrible,' she said. 'They were silvery and they were creepy. Little horns on their heads.'

Mental note to self—rem Ed mantra 1—five Ws, *Who What When Where Why*. Usually *How* as well, but doesn't apply here. Also, *Why* does not apply.

Quotes to consider: 'They were awful, their shrill piercing sound deafened me.' Mr Hourigan. 'Their wings were shiny silver when they came into the sunlight.' Mr Jones. 'One of them landed on me and I screamed. It was cold and greasy; look at my arm, it's still got a mark.' Mrs Jones.

Mental note to self—tone down witness descriptions. Ed won't like them. Plus: who is Mr Hourigan? I hear Ed ask. Include Hourigan quote, identify him first.

> The most unusual characteristic of the flying insects, said to be approximately 30cm from wingtip to wingtip, was the screaming sound they made as they fled the barn.
>
> Farmhand Jim Hourigan, who has been on the Jones farm for 27 years, told the Courier's reporter that they were an alien species.
>
> Mr and Mrs Jones did not agree, saying they were likely to be the result of experiments at the nearby CSIRO establishment.

Mental note to self—more detail needed on both Joneses and Hourigan. Rem more detail, more readers. Ed mantra 2. Esp if pictures included: Ed mantra 3.

Mental note to self—clean up wordy descriptions. Rem Ed mantra no 4: When in doubt, leave it out.

Mental note to self—get clearer description of insects for comment by university expert, bound to be one around. And CSIRO, dummy! In fact, CSIRO first.

Mental note to self—since CSIRO only 2km away, call in on way to office.

Mental note to self—scrub hands first. I resent how Mrs Jones looked askance at my ink-stained fingers (check if askance is spelled right—always learning, learning) when biro leaked after bloody tape recorder died.

Major Ed mantra #5 but should be #1—bring own notebook and pen. Pens.

Mental note to self—write civil thank you note to Mr and Mrs J for patience in finding paper and pen for me. Don't mention better pen would have been welcome.

Mental note to self—ask Ed for new recorder. Scratched and weather-worn not a professional look. I could tell Mr Jones doubted my qualifications when he saw it. Also ask for raise; old boots not good look even on farm when self is proper journalist.

EVANSDALE COURIER: FRIDAY 12 MARCH
CSIRO DENIES RESPONSIBILITY

A CSIRO spokesperson today rejected claims by local farmers that scientific experiments have led to gigantic dangerous insects.

'We don't experiment on insects,' the spokesperson said.

No verifiable evidence of the farmers' claims has been found.

629 words

THE COLOURFUL ROCK

Sebastian's dad Michael was a paleoecologist, which Sebastian knew meant his dad studied rocks and fossils and layers of stone to learn about the ancient ecology and the climate. Sebastian also knew his dad flew away in planes to faraway places and brought him back good presents like footballs and train sets and buckets of Lego.

Michael was in the cold hills adjacent to the famous Nazca desert in Peru (which Sebastian enjoyed saying because it sounded so much like 'poo') when his team came across a cache of dirt-encrusted rocks, some thirty of them, about the size of a tennis ball but more or less oval. Their roundish shape was probably caused by flowing water before they were buried, millions of years ago. One of the team of students rinsed them, turning them over and over, but they didn't seem particularly interesting and she moved them off to one side of the dig.

One of the rocks caught Michael's eye. It was basically grey, but there were streaks of blue, purple and cream. That particular combination reminded him of the basket that his mother Phoebe had made for Sebastian, beautifully crocheted in blue, purple and cream. Sebastian kept his treasures in it. The stone would match it amazingly well. Michael asked a student to put it aside for him.

Usually when Sebastian went to bed, he cuddled a squishy rubbery dog that Grandpa Rob had given him for his birthday. It was called Bluey and it fitted neatly into one hand. During the daytime, it stayed in the basket with his special things: two tiny metal elephants, one with its trunk up, one down, four shells he'd found on the beach, a rusty old lock, a dozen rocks with interesting shapes or colours, all lying on a round crocheted mat, made by Nana Phoebe. At his request, the mat was red and blue. He didn't like blue and purple much.

When Michael gave Sebastian the oval rock, his son put it in the Nana Phoebe basket but he took it out now and again just to look at it. He liked the feel of his new roundy rock, and he took it to bed one night with Bluey.

Michael didn't know that his small boy loved his new round rock so much that it gradually took Bluey's place. He took it to bed with him every night. Sebastian's mum Tina knew and she didn't mind that he fell asleep with his warm little hand wrapped around the new rock. Most nights it lay against his warm body, snug under a sheet and a blanket, never getting cold like its mates high in the hills near the Nazca desert. In Proo.

In the daytime it stayed in its matching basket, where it was kept warm by the wintery sun through the bedroom window.

One morning while Sebastian was at kindy, Tina was horrified to find a dead reptile of some kind in his bed. Clearly the oval rock had been an egg of some sort and, she thought after the first scream of shock, it was very lucky the ugly creature surrounded by broken shards of grey, purple, blue and cream was already dead because she would have crushed it herself. It could have bitten Sebby, or poisoned him!

The weird spiky creature, only a few centimetres long, seemed to have tiny wings. It was coloured much the same as the rock, or the egg, but pretty or not, it was promptly dispatched to the bin. She cleaned off the drying wet stuff on the sheets and considered binning them too, but instead left them soaking in the laundry.

She lied valiantly to her son that night—she had 'no idea where the round rock had gone', it was 'so sad', 'maybe Bluey would make him feel better'. They searched the room together and Sebastian had to settle for Bluey.

When Tina told her husband what had happened, she didn't understand the urgency of his, 'get it out of the bin at once!' He became quite agitated searching his papers for 'the exact location', of what, Tina didn't know, muttering to himself

Tina, not very happily, began scrabbling through the garbage bin, all the while scoffing silently at her husband.

A dragon indeed!

713 words

JOURNEY BACK

Gemma lay on the flat white base of the machine, which was very like an MRI scanner, waiting for the time to pass. She gazed at the faintly twinkling panel above her head, unmoving. 'You're mine,' she muttered, 'even if no one knows it but a thief.'

'90 seconds, Gemma,' a disembodied voice called, and Gemma raised a forefinger in acknowledgement.

Her recent life flashed before her eyes—appropriate really as she was facing a kind of death—and she relived the most exciting moment. Her mother waving a piece of paper at her, squealing with excitement, barely coherent. Then taking a deep breath, her mother saying solemnly, 'You have won…a trip back!'

Gemma was struck dumb. Her mother's, 'When will you go? What will you do, who will you see?' went unanswered.

Journeys back in time were always for a measly two hours. Gemma knew exactly when and where she would spend the time. She didn't have to explain her choice to those in charge: in the bureaucracy's opinion little harm could be done in two hours. Back travellers could only go into a tiny segment of their own lives and most people went back to be with loved ones. The present never seemed to be altered to any great extent.

Gemma didn't plan harm, just the rectification of an injustice. She was going back to sit a two-hour examination again, the one that should have led to a brilliant future. Instead it had been the catalyst for a life of drudgery. And it was her own fault.

Towards the end of the exam she had made the mistake of scribbling on the waste paper provided for figuring out. She had laid out her once-in-a-lifetime inspiration, the amazing formula, the unique equation sprung fully formed into her mind, the one that led to time travel—those few symbols on the back of an exam page had been stolen and developed by a brazen academic thief. Who had failed her in the exam and left her to drift into obscurity.

She had memorised that final formula but no one took any notice when she claimed ownership. She had no proof and she was regarded as mentally unstable. Now, she would fix it.

Moments later, there she was, a 38-year-old mind inside her 18-year-old self, exactly where she needed to be. She took a deep breath, feeling the difference in her whole body. She looked around the exam room, marvelling. There was Jennifer, she looked so young, and Derek, and Tom. Professor, ah, Dunstable caught her eye, frowning. Gemma put her head down and worked on the exam paper.

She raced through the exam—she had no trouble handling the science and maths—and now she was at the crucial point where she'd made her mistake ten years ago. This was when she'd spent her spare time on the waste paper, doodling calculations and equations and functions and algorithms. She'd even written 'time travel' down one side, identifying it for anyone to see.

And someone had seen it. And that someone had stolen it from her.

Now she drew on the same page. She drew trees and birds and flowers. She drew a clock—a private amusement in the situation—and she drew a river, representing the river of time which until her insight had always flowed one way.

Time was up. Exam papers were handed in. She had about two minutes before her mind would return to its 38-year-old body twenty years hence—she smoothed her skirt over her slender hips, her 18-year-old hips. Jennifer and Derek were waiting for her.

She walked with them into the corridor which led to their lockers. She listened to their chatter, smiling, waiting. They were so young! Jennifer had gone on to do valuable work but the other two had faded from public view in the years ahead. Gemma realised she'd forgotten the combination for her locker, but it wouldn't matter. She'd be gone very soon. She glanced at the watch on her slim wrist and her breath hitched. Her heart stuttered.

It was almost a full minute past the time she should have vacated this body. Not hearing Jennifer or Derek or the other students clustered about, Gemma gazed fearfully at her watch.

It was two minutes past the time. It was three minutes past. It was four minutes past.

728 words

VISITORS

Look, I promised to tell you all about it, so you don't have to threaten me.

Yeah, it'd be good if you record what I say. But don't interrupt, okay, or I'll lose track of what I'm saying.

Rightio. It all started when I got the invitation to the garden party to welcome a new ambassador to Canberra. The party was a beaut opportunity to pass on in person the message my different Visitors have been shouting at me for quite a while—oh, by the way, when you get the tape written up, please spell Visitor with a capital V, would you?—that's good, thanks. Anyway—yeah, yeah, I'll be telling you about the Visitors, just hang on.

Orright. Well, I nearly did pass on the message from the Visitors. Nearly. I had it all rehearsed, well, my current Visitor had sort of rehearsed it with me when it knew I was going to meet the ambassador.

This is what I nearly said, very fast because I didn't expect to have long to talk to such an important person as an ambassador—

'I'm pleased to meet you, your eminence' (shaking hands at this point, and planning to keep hold of his hand so he'd have to listen to me), 'and I hope you've got time to listen to me. This is the message I have from the Visitors for you: *We are circling the Earth and we will land on the White House lawn at noon on Friday the 14th January. Please bring the President.'*

Well, I think that was the date. I tried to tell them in Washington in January they'd probably be landing in snow but they didn't understand.

And if you're wondering where my present Visitor is, it's right here on my left shoulder. See the hole in the shoulder of my black coat? That's where it is. It's convenient for shouting at me. They have to shout because they're so small.

I can see you're wondering why I've had more than one Visitor. It's sad, really—they're so tiny I keep losing them. Sometimes I forget one's there and it washes off my shoulder under the shower. Then my friends keep on thinking it's a bug and flick it off when I'm working without my shirt. The first time that happened I searched the grass for half an hour before I gave up and by then of course another Visitor had arrived without me noticing.

I don't know how they know when I lose one.

One Visitor I unfortunately crushed to death with tweezers trying to relocate it to my right shoulder. People were starting to think I was odd, always whispering to my left shoulder. After that sad incident I've left them there,

Anyway, I was going to finish up by saying to the ambassador, 'I hope you'll have your President waiting on his lawn at noon on

Friday the 14th January. And I hope you enjoy your stay in our country.'

Now, as I said, that's what I *nearly* said to the ambassador. But I noticed in time that he had a translator with him and he wasn't American at all! Wasn't that lucky?

So all I actually said was, 'How'd ya do?' So the Visitor started shouting at me because I hadn't passed on the message and I had to explain to it why I hadn't said what we'd rehearsed, so your security people made me leave. And now you've probably got me on a blacklist. Undesirable person, or something like that. I've told the Visitors and told them, time and again, if you walk around talking to your left shoulder, people get suspicious but it seems I'm the only person in the whole world they've found who can hear them, no matter how loud they shout.

The funny thing is I've been deaf in my left ear since I was born!

What's most annoying is that the Visitors won't accept that I've had my only chance at talking to such an important person as an ambassador, so they'll go on shouting their message at me until I go crazy or they bomb the Earth with their tiny bombs!

After all, it must have been pure luck this time. How often can a plain gardener be included by mistake on a list of people to welcome a new ambassador to the country?

730 words

MOTHER

'One thing I'm having trouble with is the concept of *mother.*'

I am talking with an adult Fern, whose name in English is something like Beggleton. There are a couple of gurgles in the middle of the name, but plain *Beggleton* seems to be acceptable to him. He presents himself as male; that makes things easier. A people with three genders will be difficult to get my head around; I haven't met a third gender person yet. As far as I know.

Beggleton says, ‘I know every birth requires a male and a female parent—I had them myself after all—but in your world, your culture, a female parent is more than just the life-bearer. Am I right?’

I’m here to learn about his culture, his society. Beggleton is unusual in being so curious about humans. Usually his people don’t find us particularly interesting.

We hope that raising our human children here will make the interface between humans and these humanoid aliens easier in future. Not that Beggleton’s people are the aliens, of course. That’s us. Me. The alien human.

‘Before I talk about that, would you remind me how your people give birth?’ I ask

An aquatic people, the natives of this planet can stay underwater for a long time but like our whales, they must surface for air regularly. We call them Ferns and they don’t seem to dislike it. The gills they use underwater are under a fine fern-like fringe around the neck.

The Ferns are born in water and stay there until they can survive on land, much like humans inside the watery womb of their mothers. Unlike humans, the Ferns copulate only once. They do it in the darkness of mid-winter, under thick ice without ever knowing each other. In a state quite close to hibernation, their bodies go through the process without their minds being involved at all. There are male and female, and offspring result from the sightless matings under the ice. They don’t know exactly what happens under the ice; they survive, and the young appear.

There were marine creatures on old Earth that reproduced by casting sperm across the water willy-nilly. Maybe the Ferns do the same.

Some human scientists are pressing for underwater cameras to witness the mating and the genesis of the young, but others, successfully so far, want to wait for the Ferns to suggest it. They’ll come to it someday.

Those young who survive that first winter under the ice grow rapidly on land with the return of a warmer season. They gather in groups and adults feed them and look after them until they develop intelligence and become independent.

They only return to the icy depths when they are mature and feel the urge to reproduce. Once. Beggleton has not had his copulatory adventure yet.

No wonder the idea of 'mother' in human terms is so foreign.

For humans, I tell Beggleton, the maternal bond—whether biological or adopted (though I don't go into that)—is arguably the strongest, most important relationship in a child's early years. A healthy attachment with a loving primary caregiver (mother, father, or both) that fosters trust and affection will often dictate how secure and confident we feel later in life.

Of course, I tell him, not everyone is so fortunate. The troubles experienced by many adult humans can be traced back to deficiencies in the parenting. Not every woman carries the innate desire to build maternal bonds or the mental well-being to provide the security and stability that children need.

All this time, Beggleton and I have been sitting opposite each other. We are in a recording studio and there is a small audience of both humans and Ferns. The attention of the Ferns is rather unnerving, as they all, without exception, stare at my belly the whole time.

Beggleton asks, 'Did you have a loving and supportive mother?

I think back with affection. I have been so blessed compared with many others. I nod, and smile. 'And father too. I was lucky.'

'Will you be a loving and supportive mother?'

Suddenly my child moves, and my belly ripples. I pat my abdomen, which is stretched out ahead of me as I sit with my legs splayed to give it room. It is so big, so round, so firm, so full of baby only days away from arriving.

Beggleton springs to his feet and stumbles backwards, spluttering. The Ferns are on their feet, alarmed.

'It's okay,' I say, 'he's not coming out right this minute.'

756 words

Frances Goodey

SAME TIME NEXT WEEK

Isabella looked around the lab, down at her white lab coat, around the lab again. Very happily. All Izzy ever wanted to do was science.

And now she would. She was on tenterhooks, anxious, like the other two students, to learn the big secret. Sam and Evie were as much in the dark as she was. Common gossip whispered that students had to swear to secrecy about what they learned here; no one had ever been known to break the oath they swore.

She concentrated on Professor Halliwell as he sat on the edge of his desk, one foot swinging as he studied their faces. His grey-flecked hair and short beard added maturity to his otherwise youthful features as he addressed them.

They were joining an elite group, he told them. Every two years three students were chosen, appointed, to join the team. If they did, they would learn things they could never talk about to other people. In fact—he produced three sheets of paper.

The Official Secrets Act. His serious face changed to a stern one. Even if they left in the next 20 minutes, they would have heard something that they could never tell anyone. Sign here. They all signed.

The military paid for everything in the lab, everything he and his teams came up with. If anyone felt they couldn't handle that, if the idea of the defence forces of their country being in charge of their lives forever more—very comfortable cosy lives though they could be—then they had better leave, right now.

But they could never talk about it. Life in prison could result if they told people about it.

Was that the big secret? It must be. Izzy had never suspected the military had a hand in anything at the university. She'd never heard gossip or chat about it. It must be the big secret.

She thought rapidly. The military meant big money behind whatever research was conducted here. She would use her brain, she would be doing real science, she didn't care if it was the military behind everything. She signed.

Evie and Sam both left the room with the professor's words following them out the door: not only don't tell anyone, don't discuss it, wipe it from your minds. Tell people whatever you want, just don't mention the military.

Isabel and the professor looked at each other. He beckoned her to follow him and they went into a small inner room she'd barely noticed.

A bench on the back wall held a variety of machines. Professor Halliwell pointed at a high stool placed in front of one of them, a metre-tall glass and dials contraption unlike anything she'd seen before. She sat and looked up at him.

'We study time travel,' he said. Izzy laughed. He wasn't known for a sense of humour but that was funny.

'We study time travel,' he said again. 'This is where I convince you.'

Izzy's smile faded. Lord, was he crazy? He placed a hand on her shoulder in reassurance. 'I know time travel is a physical and scientific impossibility, it's physiologically unfeasible, no way, no how, can't be done.'

Izzy was so uncomfortable. What had she let herself in for?

'Quantum physics, those tiny bits that puzzle us all, quantum physics lets us travel in time, just not with our bodies. Calm down, Isabel, I'm not nuts.'

After a half hour of talking, explaining, convincing, Izzy agreed to face that tall glass machine, to stare into a certain segment without blinking—then she balked. Professor Halliwell agreed to do it first.

She watched him stare into the machine and a moment later, watching over his shoulder, she saw a fuzzy image on another nearby screen. It cleared. It was Professor Halliwell, dressed for winter, carrying a pair of skis over one shoulder, holding the hand of a small boy, similarly dressed.

'I'm on holiday next week,' he said. 'The whole family is going skiing. I just saw myself, exactly one week in the future. This time of day, one week away.'

He turned to her. 'It *is* time travel, we look into the future, but we have to expand it enormously for it to have any benefit. Now, your turn.'

As she took his place on the stool, he said, 'Once you see yourself, you'll be convinced.'

She sure would, she thought, peering into the glass, aware of him adjusting dials.

The screen flickered and whirred. The screen stayed dark. Isabel took a deep breath.

'I'm not here next week.'

757 words

ELQIL PIE

You want to know how it is I own a chain of restaurants? Where did my wealth come from? It's an interesting story, unique really.

When I was 21, I was apprentice chef on the interspace liner *Freedom Shift*, the name supposedly suggesting a fantastic future for passengers with a bit of science thrown in. I dunno. It was just where I worked.

My boss, the head chef, was a Bulgarian of all things and what he didn't know about cooking for hundreds of people wasn't worth knowing. I got on well with him and he asked me one day if I wanted to visit the galley on another ship, the Vistron vessel *Green Sky*.

I accepted at once. I'd only met one Vistron before and I'd love to see what they ate. And cooked. I made sure my active memory device was switched on. I wouldn't want to forget any new cooking techniques I might see.

The Vistrons are humanoid so of course they breathe the air that we breathe, and their bodies work much like ours. The third ear behind their necks gives them amazing hearing as you might imagine, but the sixth finger on each hand doesn't do much for them, or so I thought at first.

Anyway, when we visited, I was ferried off to the junior staff while my boss socialised with his peers. I ended up spending most time with Arkood, a young Vistron who was an apprentice cook like me. He was good company. He found me a mildly stimulating drink—I had three in the end—and he invited me to help prepare part of the next meal on board.

Turns out a sixth finger is pretty helpful when you have to thinly slice a trengoil eel. They're slippery little buggers. I nearly ended up with only four fingers on one hand. But it was fun, and I was able to show Arkood a trick or two with the vegetables that he hadn't seen before. He looked forward to showing his boss.

The main job he got me to help with was making an elqil pie. I'd never heard of it. It involved kneading and flattening a big lump of crek which was a rare kind of soil from their planet. It seemed to me an odd thing to have in a kitchen, but Arkood explained.

Crek had the ability to pull the mild toxin from the flesh of a saltwater fish from his planet, I think the fish was called stox'ox, something like that, and left untreated it could make people ill. The stox'ox was cooked wrapped in the crek, which was later discarded.

The name of the pie came from the elqils that were scattered at random throughout the crek. They had to be removed before the cooking.

As soon as I started kneading the crek, I found elqils. I found three at once, all a pretty turquoise, and I picked them out and showed them to Arkood. He said just put them aside, he'd put them in the garbage in a minute. Only cooks ever got to see elqils because they were the only ones to have a use for crek.

I found thirteen more elqils, pink, greenish-blue, orange, yellow. I thought maybe you could put a hole in them and string them to make a bracelet or a necklace. My mother would love one. I asked Arkood if I could have them.

He said sure, the elqils are just rubbish. He pointed out a bag with its top open at one end of a preparation bench. It was full of the glassy elqils, along with the lumps of crek that had been cooked already. I bent to have a sniff but there wasn't much smell at all, not fishy as I expected. At a quick glance I could see dozens of the elqils. All sorts of colours. There was a deep purple one that I thought I wouldn't mind in a ring for myself.

I asked Arkood if I could take the whole bag of crek with me. Dispose of it for him and maybe pick out some of the elqils? He just shrugged, probably thought I was crazy wanting a bag of garbage, but he didn't care.

I didn't tell my boss, or anyone, that I had it, but during the rest of the trip I went through that crek with scrupulous care and ended up with more than a hundred Vistron elqils. Back on earth, I discovered they were better than diamonds in all sorts of ways, including their value. Which increased exponentially when the Vistron world was overrun by the Cinzets forty years ago.

So, I was a very wealthy young man at the end of that spaceliner's run. I never found out what happened to Arkood and I never got to taste the elqil pie. I wish I had.

815 words

FINAL LIST

The men finding seats in the airconditioned room were in varied uniforms. As three men in business suits settled themselves at a desk up front, chairs shifted, people coughed and murmured, waiting.

Automatically most reached for the tablets in front of them, turning them on.

Terry Randolph sat in the back row, in his tan trainee astronaut outfit. He tugged the short sleeve over the irritating patch on his upper arm. He was surrounded by a sea of grey and blue, technical, medical, backup, support. They seem to have sprouted like leaves in spring.

'Guys, I've called you here to break some bad news.' Pete Landon didn't look comfortable.

Terry looked around. He'd said 'guys', and while the word was largely gender neutral, it appeared to be accurate. Not a female in sight. Though he could be wrong. Some of the women were indistinguishable from their male colleagues once in uniform, especially with the shorn heads so many of them had. Terry ran his hand across his skull—another week and he'd need to shave it again. He liked the convenience of a bald head. If he ever made it into space, he'd consider having it all permanently removed.

He was absent-mindedly rubbing the therapeutic arm patch when Pete said, 'I want you to open the site Mark's going to put up. It's a brief history lesson.'

Mark Marsden hauled his overweight body out of his seat and scribbled a web address on the whiteboard. The site was a specially-prepared spiel about the history of females in space, specifically why NASA barred women from the beginning. Which they knew wasn't true, but they obediently skimmed the text and watched the film clips.

In the late 50s, NASA began considering how to recruit astronauts. After first contemplating a public invitation to apply, they realised far too many people would do so, and processing all the applications was going to be lengthy and costly. Why not use military test pilots? This not only kept the numbers down, but it was a group that was fit, educated and had security clearance. The question of whether to accept women as astronauts never even came up as there were no female military test pilots—because the US military didn't accept women into pilot training.

Different story today, Terry thought, with a silent chuckle. Like Ginger Rogers famously said, anything men can do, women can do—backwards and in high heels. Terry thought of another proviso he'd heard recently: they also do it bleeding.

'And now this, gentlemen. You're the first to see it.' Pete Landon sounded serious. *This* was a secure NASA site which they all opened with personal passwords.

At last! The list of eligible applicants for the permanent Mars expedition, looked like hundreds of names. Listed by last name.

After two successful landings and returns from Mars, a group of 200 would be going to Mars and staying there. They'd be safe from fierce solar radiation, living in underground caverns with habitats and agricultural areas already established. With such a big number going, Terry knew he had a good chance to be among the lucky ones. A trained astronaut with a medical degree, he ought to be a shoo-in.

He couldn't see his name. He turned back a screen. Though there was something about the list…

He noticed the noise level rising. People were sounding agitated. 'What's up?' he said to his nearest neighbour.

The man turned his screen towards Terry. 'They're all women.'

'What?' Terry turned to his own screen. He was right. Mary, Nancy, Patricia, Leonore, Madeleine, Suzanne, Freda, Rosemary, Olga…

Pete Landon hammered the desk for silence and gradually the voices simmered down. Terry stopped himself from nervously rubbing his arm patch.

'You know that women have consistently outshone men on all the physical and psychological tests for space flight.' Pete looked around at the intent male faces. 'You all know that groups of women consistently prove to be more compatible over time during periods of deprivation. No one can claim women don't qualify for any job you care to name. I'm sure you all know that testosterone gets jobs done but it doesn't keep people safe or contented.'

He held up a hand to forestall the squawks that were beginning. 'There's a clincher that can't be ignored.'

Into the silence he said, 'Babies.'

Pete Landon looked around the stunned faces. 'You can all donate your sperm, gentlemen, but you can't carry a baby and you can't deny that mothering takes mothers.'

In the ensuing hubbub, Terry was rubbing his therapeutic patch when Brian Lane smacked his shoulder. 'You'll be right, mate.' He slapped Terry's arm, right on the patch, and grinned at him. 'It's not too late for you to get your name on the list. You can always be Teresa again. Nothing irreversible's been done, has it?'

Terry glared at him. 'I never was Teresa, you idiot. How about you volunteer to become Brianna, or Bryony?'

Brian sat back and shrugged. 'No way. Not even for Mars.'

839 words

THE LATE PHONE CALL

'Mrs Grace? Mrs Grace?'

That's me. I sit a bit straighter and look around. Matron Spender is right in front of me and behind her, visible because they're much taller, are two uniformed men. They're smiling, so I guess that's good.

Ten minutes later the two Captains, Miles and Roger—first names are fine, we feel we know you through your brother, one of them says—they're having coffee with me at the common room table. I hope their seats are comfortable. I'm still in my wheelchair. The younger one is looking at me with awe. I know awe when I see it. I remember it on my own face when I learned Jake was going into space.

I was 14 when he vanished into the great beyond. 90 years ago. I remember it so well, that final kiss and hug, and his promise of regular contact. Time-delayed of course, the further he and his crew went, but contact all the same.

Paying attention, I reply to one question, 'The last time I had a message from Jake was in 2042, ten years after they left. I was 24, just graduated—I still have a copy somewhere. He looked very young I remember.' I smile at the two young men. 'Nowadays, everyone's young to me.' Pre-empting a likely question, I add, 'I'm 104 next month.'

Miles leans towards me. 'Mrs Grace, did you ever sign the Official Secrets Act?'

'What an odd question! But no, I don't believe I ever did. Why?'

The other man, Roger, produces some pages from his briefcase and places them before me, with a pen. How old-fashioned! Why not on-screen, I wonder, but he's talking.

'We have something to show you, something related to your brother Jacob. But you must sign the Official Secrets Act first. You may not talk to anyone about what we'll show you.' He looks around the common room. 'You'll notice we're alone. Even Matron Spender is barred from the room just now.'

Well, this is interesting. I look over pages rather full of legal-looking paragraphs and look up at the men. Miles says, 'Basically you'll go to prison if you talk.' He smiles. 'But I guess we can expect you to be a model citizen.'

I bounce the pen in my hand—so long since I've seen one—and sign: Eleanor Mary Grace. 'Now, what's up?'

Roger goes to the screen on the wall and inserts a disc. Miles says, 'Mrs Grace, may I hold your hand while you watch? No bad intentions, I promise, just support for you. It may be upsetting.'

'I'm a tough old bird, but yes, we can hold hands.' He grins at the change of meaning. Roger returns as the screen lights up, and there's Jake, so very, very young.

Roger pauses it and I gaze at Jake as Miles talks. Jake's grinning with his shoulders lifted, as though caught in a shrug. 'It was never revealed to the public,' Miles says, 'that your brother's spaceship has never stopped sending its location, in all the 80 years since it stopped communicating. So we've always known where, exactly which planet, it's on—and now we have a message.'

'It's not recent, surely? Jake's so young, and it's been so long.'

'We'll leave it to the brainiacs to work out time difference, time dilation, all that stuff. We want you to watch this. At the end you'll know why you can't talk about it.'

So I settle back.

It's as though I were 24 again. Jake talks about inconsequential things. His exercise routine, their diet, wishing he knew how old I was and hoping my life is good. Don't forget to name a son after him. I find myself nodding. I did that. My boy Jacob is long gone.

Reminding me to give his best wishes to an old friend on his birthday. Then he looks serious. They'll be landing soon, looks like a planet with both water and air fit for humans. Then, in the background, there's a commotion. Two of Jake's crew barrel across the room behind him, shouting indistinctly. Jake turns sharply away from the camera.

I glance at Miles and Roger but they're watching intently.

Now, Jake turns back to the camera and my heart jolts as I hear him say, 'This might be my last phone call, sis. I love you,' and something flashes from left to right behind him. It's gold and glowing—it could be an upright bar of gold but it's not, it's a creature, its figure is supple, pliable, leaning forward—and off screen in an instant—and Jake's hand reaches, and the screen goes dark.

He must have touched the 'send' button. And it sent. His final phone call.

I release a breath I didn't know I was holding. Miles is squeezing my hand. 'I'm okay,' I say to him.

'We have a print. Do you want to see it? You can't keep it though.'

When I nod, Roger hands me a large colour print of the golden creature. Its face is caught clearly, it's human, humanoid, human-looking anyway, and it's smiling.

855 words

Frances Goodey

THE UGLY ALIENS

The first day, the very first time, I saw the aliens, with my own eyes, I felt sorry for them. *You'd feel sorry for a mongrel dog*, I could imagine my dad saying. Well, he'd be right.

They were lying listlessly on rough pallets covered by something like hessian, very uncomfortable-looking bedding. But these aren't mongrel dogs. They're unknown creatures, new to science, new to the world, like nothing we've ever seen, ever.

Their spaceship was tracked by the Tidbinbilla Deep Space scientists, so they knew where it landed, on 'an isolated patch of desert in the Australian outback'—that's what the TV people said. They all thought it was a meteorite, but it wasn't.

I'm a cleaner, not much education to my name, but I read, and I think, and I know you don't treat intelligent creatures like this. They must be intelligent, travelling through space and all.

They looked ugly enough on TV and in the flesh they're even uglier—a bit like the gremlins in that movie, but more hideous. Greenish-blue mostly with dull brown patches here and there. Rough spiky skin, eyes I guess, somewhere in the folds of the upper part of the body. Funny tendril-looking things always waving about. No bigger than a newborn kitten.

It's not right to have them lying on that scratchy coarse stuff even if they are aliens. They might be horrible-looking but I felt sorry for them. I feel sorry for them.

I've got the key for their enclosure, but I'm not allowed in to clean for them, but there's only three of them and they're so little and limp—I'm gonna go in and give them a cuddle.

#

I'm standing in front of the Commander's desk, feeling ten years old. Caught out, embarrassed. 'I feel sorry for them,' I tell him. 'They're so little and far away from their home.'

'Actually, their home is about 20 metres away.' I hate it when smart people show off with comments that mean a lot to them, but I don't understand. So I stare at him.

'We've got their spaceship here in a secret underground floor that you haven't needed to know about.'

'Really?' I feel pleased. 'Can they go back to it?'

'Maybe,' he says. 'Look, Ron, I want to tell you about it. Let's have a bit less formality and relax a bit.'

A few minutes later I'm having a chummy cup of coffee with him, sitting opposite him on a cosy lounge chair with a shiny wooden coffee table between us.

It turns out that if the little aliens are placed on a smooth surface they scamper all over the place. It's only when they're on a coarse surface, like hessian, that they keep still. And, they've discovered I'm the only person the Commander's seen that the aliens haven't buzzed with electricity. No one else can touch them easily!

#

The experts want to try an experiment. Would I consider taking one of the aliens into the spaceship to see what happens? They'd have cameras and voice connections and so forth. I don't mind. I like the little aliens. It will be interesting to see their home.

Going to fetch one of them, I feel strange. It feels as though someone's trying to talk to me, but I don't understand. It's like when I went deaf for a few months when I was a kid. I know someone's talking but I can't make it out. I look around but there's only the Commander and me.

In the enclosure I say to the Commander, I don't know why, right out of the blue, 'I want to take all three with me.'

He thought about it for a moment and nodded. I feel happy about it.

Sure enough, the spaceship is there in its special hidden-away space. I get fitted up with vision and sound equipment and carry the three little aliens inside. It's so clean, creamy white surfaces with bench-type furniture around the walls. Some of them are covered in a soft cushiony-looking material so I sit on one and put the aliens beside me. They don't move.

I get the urge to put them on the floor. The floors a mess. It's smooth and shiny but very grubby. The scientists have left shoe prints everywhere. I put the little aliens on the floor and they wake right up. Two of them whiz around the floor and the shoe prints disappear. One of them goes right up the wall and I look up. There's a black smear—someone must have tested a crayon or something—and the little alien cleans it right up!

They aren't aliens at all! Well they are, but they're also automatic cleaners. Little vacuum cleaners. I laugh out loud.

I hear a voice inside my head. It's saying, 'thank you', and 'please leave now', and 'goodbye'.

I get out just in time. The spaceship is already making a buzzing sound as the door closes behind me. Then the ship slowly rotates, then turns faster and faster and tunnels its way up through the floors of the science centre, and then it's gone.

I wonder if the scientists will believe the spaceship talked to me.

871 words

STORIES WITH WORD COUNT 886-5292

FERAL

I could hear Skye screaming my name before she arrived. Knowing my nursing skills could be needed—because the nearest doctor was a full 45 minutes drive away—I rushed outside to see a straggling line of the cousins running wildly behind Skye, a wave of yells and cries preceding them. No adults. I squeezed Skye's shoulders, wincing at her shrieking.

I'd been quietly revising material for tomorrow's exam. The family were all out for a final look around before we headed home. I'd managed quite a bit of study, amazing when three adults and five kids filled the cabin.

My brothers had taken their kids camping so I'd had the place to myself and now I'd packed everything up and was waiting for them to return. Ricky and Tom had been good about my non-participation—I didn't need to be involved in every detail of the walks, swims, tree climbs and camps to be useful. I cooked, provided overnight meal packs, supervised kids' kitchen duty, swam, and played with the kids. And studied.

Now—crying, shouting, upset children.

'What is it? What's happened?'

Skye took a deep breath and raised tear-filled eyes to me. By now the other kids were arriving, streaks of blood all over, dirtied and scratched. I ushered them inside, asking, 'What the hell's going on? Where's Ricky? Where's Tom?'

Skye looked at the others, whose screams and crying were replaced by frantic panting. Olivia and Eloise were huddled on the floor, hugging each other, weeping. I knelt to embrace them and looked up at Skye. Ben and Jacob pressed against her.

'It was the sheep.'

Skye's words prompted the others and there was a chorus of, 'yes, sheep, the sheep'.

I felt my brain flip-flop and an utterly inappropriate laugh nearly burst from me—who'd ever suspect sheep?

I remembered a couple of lines from a sci fi novel about dragons. *Do you know how many people are killed by sharks each year? Less than five. And how many by cows? More than 20.... nobody ever suspects cows.*

I swallowed hard and stood. 'Tell me clearly what's happened.' I looked around at them. 'First, Jacob and Eloise, go into the office and phone the police and the ambulance. Stay together and make sure you speak clearly. If necessary, take turns to talk if they think you're pranking them. I'll come if necessary. Go!'

They took off. Holding little Olivia's hand, I turned back to Skye. 'Talk.'

I began cleaning bloodied scratches and applying ointment and band aids to torn skin.

Skye began, 'Dad and Uncle Tom were standing with us at the fence and we were looking at the sheep in the paddock.'

I nodded. I knew where she meant.

'There were about ten or 15 of them and we were having one last visit. They were all very woolly, it's nearly shearing time.' The others were nodding. 'One of them came to the fence, a big one, with thick wool, and we were leaning over and feeling the wool. It was dark on the outside and pure white inside. It was interesting.'

She took another deep breath. 'Then it turned its head and bit Dad's hand.' She gulped. 'Then it pulled Dad by the arm right over the fence and other sheep came and …' Skye shuddered.

Ben took over. 'Uncle Tom jumped over the fence and Jacob and I followed him. We were chasing after the sheep that had Dad—he got away from it but it knocked him over— and we heard screaming from behind and two other sheep had broken the fence down and were chasing the girls.'

Tears threatened to spill from his eyes. 'Uncle Tom shouted at Jacob and me to go back and when we ran back, two sheep outside were attacking the girls,' he looked at his cousin and sister—'and then one attacked us.' Jacob nodded and copying Ben, he pulled up sleeves and trouser legs to show the results. 'And then,' Ben continued, 'they suddenly turned and ran back into the paddock. By that time Uncle Tom was helping Dad, and they shouted at all of us to get out. So we did and ran back here.'

Jacob said solemnly, 'I saw Uncle Tom punch a sheep on the face.'

Bloody hell. Feral sheep.

I organised a round of warm drinks, hugged and reassured the kids who were all a bit shaky, understandably, and when Eloise and Jacob reported both police and ambulance were on the way, I made a restoring coffee for myself.

I was the only adult and there wasn't much I could do at all except mind the kids and wait for help. But where were my brothers?

I vaguely remembered hearing that animals had been released by protestors at the nearby Animal Research Laboratory, on the radio I thought, I didn't remember it on TV. No moving images, no TV. Were the sheep escapees from a Frankenstein-style genetic disaster?

Olivia started sobbing loudly. 'Where's Dad? And Uncle Ricky?' Crikey. Where were they? Maybe nearly back here. We all rushed over to the kitchen window that faced the paddock next door where usually docile sheep passed innocuous lives. My nieces and nephews crowded around me, the bigger ones embracing the smaller ones.

All we could see was sheep.

886 words

Frances Goodey

DANCING ON THE BEACH

There was one name that cropped up in succeeding generations of the Cale family, and that was Henry. There were Henrys galore—grandfathers, great- and great-great grandfathers, uncles, cousins, babies, teens, old men, scattered around the world. Many were Cales, but with other surnames too when the Cale women married and took their husbands' names.

When George Cale and his wife Rosemary had a little girl, they called her Charlotte. *Charlotte* went well with *Cale*. Then they had a second little girl, not a boy who could be named Henry. This second little girl, in the expectation of no more children for George and Rosemary, was named Henrietta.

Henrietta, known as Hetty.

Hetty Cale shared more than her name with many of her relations. A physical characteristic that cropped up in many of the family was an amazingly good sharp vision.

Hetty's mother Rosemary had investigated it when she learned about this facet of her husband's family. She learned some interesting things. It was she who told Hetty about some Australian Aboriginal people who had amazingly sharp sight. 1840s Aboriginal descriptions of constellations of stars couldn't be understood by scientists at the time. When later astronomers looked with binoculars, suddenly they could pick out all the missing stars that the Aboriginal people could see just with the naked eye.

'That's how good your vision is too,' Rosemary told Hetty.

To Hetty, it was nothing special. Her close-up vision was fine, her long-distance vision was superb. It wasn't any particular advantage as far as Hetty could tell.

Until the day Charlotte and Hetty were dancing on the beach.

Their primary school was staging a musical mermaid extravaganza, to raise money, and the girls were practising their singing and their dancing on the beach, which their family had to themselves. The day was sunny but cool and no one else came to the beach.

The girls had put on their mermaid pretend-bikini-top outfits over their swimming togs (Hetty thought it was a shame Charlotte's bright purple togs showed), each with a long skirt shaped like a tail fluttering around their ankles (the long slits up past their knees allowing for hearty kicks when needed), and their wigs of hair to the waist (one bright orange, one bright yellow) shining brightly in the spring sunshine.

The fine sandy stretch was broken up by flat slabs of grey granite and this was where the girls practised. They sang to the waves and turned to sing to their parents, 60 metres up the beach; they danced and bowed and practised their hand movements as though making their way through the sea.

Waves crashed and flowed and sprayed at the far end of a belt of flat stone extending into the sea at their end of the beach.

Then Charlotte stubbed her big toe badly enough to bleed, so she limped back to her parents, leaving a trail of red dots. Hetty stayed to practise one song in particular, which required plenty of arm actions while standing still. She shouted her song into the blue waves, gazing straight out.

When three figures jumped up out of the sea onto the last stone slab, Hetty saw them at once. Someone else might have thought they were sea lions but Hetty could see quite clearly who and what they were.

The big one was a woman, bare on her top half, with long pale greenish hair. She had a nasty scar from forehead to ear that crossed one eye, which appeared damaged. The other eye was green with lavish lashes that blinked slowly as she settled on the rock. The others were two little girls. One of them lay on her back and the other girl spread the first one's hair out flat behind her. The woman leaned over her and was using a cutter of some sort, Hetty thought it was a round scallop shell, to cut the hair short. Both girls' hair was a stronger green than the woman's.

As the girl lay back and as the other girl moved about and as the woman, the mother, moved too, all three tails flopped up and down and sideways, swishing through the air. Shiny silvery scales-on-scales tails.

Hetty looked back at Charlotte and her parents, but they were oblivious, minding Charlotte.

The second girl, mermaid, was looking Hetty's way, and raised a hand to shade her eyes. Without thinking, Hetty did the same.

The mermaid's eyes widened, and she turned to the others. They all pushed up on their hands and faced her. Hetty kept one hand shading her eyes and gave a little wave with her other hand. The two little mermaids waved back, big smiles on their faces. The mother turned and said something to them and faced Hetty again.

The mother gave a little wave too, then placed a finger on her lips. Hetty did the same, making a promise never to tell. She did a thumbs-up and in a moment all three did the same .

In an instant they twisted away and leapt back into the water.

Hetty never told anyone.

Hetty never told anyone why she urgently wanted to become a good swimmer.

Hetty, grown up, never told anyone why she ran fishing boats with the logo of a mermaid who had a finger on her lips and a thumbs-up in front of her.

893 words

CHEILITT BULBS AND KHTEAU PODS

'You need to understand,' the Oordli said, 'that humans are different.'

The Ram'n'li, who considered herself both worldly-wise and sophisticated, looked the green Oordli up and down and turned her head its full 180 degrees to inspect her own flenberri colour. 'Who isn't?'

The strongest emotion an Oordli hostel manager would allow itself in public was impatience, but it responded with restraint for the Ram'n'li was a good worker and not unintelligent, 'I do not mean physically, of course.'

The Oordli busied itself with the computer. It had been unsettled by the arrival of the human who was an unusual being. Abnormally tall, it had a disturbing amount of growth on its head. This growth appeared to have a life of its own, waving about when the human moved its head. There was a similar kind of growth about its lower face though it was a different colour. Strange.

The Ram'n'li would normally wait respectfully until a superior was ready to converse but curiosity made her ask, 'I only saw it for a moment. Why is it here on Soash?'

'Hmm.' The Oordli thought for a moment. 'He is male, by the way. He is here to work.' It paused. 'I understand he plans to stay for some time. It's less expensive to stay in a hostel when one is unemployed.'

'Of course.'

'I am having some difficulty finding the appropriate accommodation for him. He is so tall.'

'The human's height doesn't concern me,' the Ram'n'li said, 'it's feeding him that may be a problem. He must eat six times the amount of normal people. He is enormous!'

Nodding in agreement, the Oordli looked thoughtful. 'Yes, food. Yes. I said we could accommodate his food requirements.' He looked up at her, and she was gazing at him not with anger or annoyance but with bright-eyed expectation. The Ram'n'li had not been the hostel's kitchen manager for long so the Oordli was not sure what this meant. It would be good if she appreciated a challenge. 'Will you be able to meet his food requirements? Can you feed him?'

'I will examine the universal guide. Humans have been known about for quite some time now even though they don't travel in great numbers. There's bound to be some information.'

They parted, the Ram'n'li heading to her small office at the back of the kitchen. The hostel provided bed and food for a variety of species, some of them fascinating to her. She enjoyed the task most times.

She passed the tiny entrance to the tunnel through the hostel's walls that led to the isolated gas-filled set of rooms that hosted, currently, three little representatives of Chorkla. Not many hostels would go to the expense of providing what guests like the Chorklans needed. Only Chorklans could survive on Chorkla but luckily for them they could undertake intergalactic travel if they had their personal breathing apparatus.

The Ram'n'li wondered briefly if the gas-filled suite would be emptied for other species once the Chorklans were gone. But first, the human, and its, his, food.

Deep in study of the universal guide, the Ram'n'li was discovering that not much was known about the food habits of humans. Surely the normal provisions of vegetation from the very wide range available to her would suffice. She had access to the little airy sacs of the cheilitt tree that the Zapgreeb loved, though half the time they seemed to ingest only the air. So many cheilitt bulbs littered the floor after the Zapgreeb left the room! Maybe the human would like them. That would be economical indeed.

Every species she knew of could eat the very filling khteau pods. Some folks ate only the khteau! Fortunately, they grew everywhere.

Drinks now. Water of course the human must have. She would simply have to talk to him about his food. Water and bread were basic, a good start. She had breads of every description on hand of course, and most folks could eat them. Well, the Ugriws couldn't of course. She had a handy stock of krohee frozen for them. Perhaps the human …

The bell from the Oordli's desk rang. And once again. That was a direct summons.

Standing in front of the desk was a uniformed Customs official. It was a local, a Soashan. Like all Soashans it did not allow its diminutive size to be what people noticed about it. Like all Soashans, it saw itself as the tallest creature in any room.

The Oordli said rather loudly (trying to impress the Soashan, the Ram'n'li thought), 'My kitchen manager. Please tell her what you have told me.'

The Soashan looked up at the Ram'n'li and spat its words with a hissing sibilance that filled the room. 'Customs has decided that the human's contraband may be returned to him. It is an item of food, unknown in Soash, but tests have found it harmless.'

The Ram'n'li stood motionless as the Soashan's sibilant spittle coated her lower legs. She had forgotten this about Soashans. She had to say something, had to ignore the wetness trickling down her legs. 'Oh? What exactly is it, what kind of food? May I see it?'

The Soashan opened its satchel, its fourth hand holding it away from its body. 'Its outer shell is made from the lining of an animal's stomach—' the Ram'n'li recoiled—'it has many preservative chemicals but is safe to eat, even for us. It has collagen and cellulose but basically it is cleaned animal intestines—'

Shock electrified the Ram'n'li—'while the inner part is the flesh of an earth animal.'

The Ram'n'li fainted.

She didn't see the tall lumbering human arrive, or see him peering past the Soashan, or hear his words. 'That's my frankfurter. Have you got the second one?'

965 words

A MINOR MYSTERY

A single raucous cry startles Luke and he sprawls onto the stones, landing on one knee. He scowls first at the crow low on the scribbly gum, then at the knee of his jeans. It's dusty but luckily not torn: sewing isn't one of his talents.

He continues running, more aware of the road surface, enjoying the physical challenge of the run, the eucalyptus filling the air, planning his next few hours.

He'd waved his parents off, his young sister pulling faces at him through the car window and now he has the week to himself. He must pay for the privilege by cleaning up the cabin, stocking the wood box, checking the dish.

He glances at the Randall house, checking the direction of the satellite dish on its roof. Due north. Right. Mum and Dad and Sophie would watch TV sometimes. Hopefully he wouldn't have to climb up on the roof of the cabin to adjust the dish. Accidents do happen. Imagine if he'd twisted an ankle or, god forbid, had broken a leg with that little fall back there.

He'd dig out the fishing gear once he'd swept the floors and dug out the bed linen. He jogs on.

A figure appears in a window at the Randalls. Dad said the old couple didn't use it much, but there's someone there. He raises a hand without thinking and the person vanishes.

Shrugging the minor mystery away, he enjoys the stately gum trees, and their eucalyptus scent. He is calm and contented, just where he wants to be.

Two hours later, Luke isn't quite as satisfied. The generator works, thanks to Dad. The water tank is full. The floors are swept, the right number of sheets and blankets are waving in the breeze as the dust of months fall out of them—Mum had said they were all clean, they only needed airing. Just as well. Washing them all would take forever.

But this damned satellite dish! Gingerly using the old ladder, its feet jammed into holes in the ground, he checks the state of the dish. It seems okay, but the picture on the screen tells another story. It looks as though adjusting the dish might do the trick but he's going to be up and down like a yoyo getting it right. While there's daylight.

Binoculars slung around his neck, Luke is going to align his dish with the Randall dish. Luckily, it's visible through the trees filling the valley between the houses. Hopefully their dish is aligned right. If not—yoyo time.

Two wallabies are lounging in the shade under the gums and directly below Luke a baby koala peeks out from its mother pouch. He grins at it, thinking Sophie would love it and shakes his head. Back to work! He raises the binoculars.

There's a crowd inside the Randall place! No cars or SUVs though. How strange. Looking more closely, Luke can't make out much. There are dark impressions, people-shaped figures, that ebb and flow inside the two windows he can see. Then one appears at the side of the house. Luke's mouth gapes as he steadies his binoculars on the person who appears to flow up the side of the house to its roof. No ladder. Just up and up and over.

His breathing ragged, Luke finetunes the focus. The figure is black. Not black clothing or hair or—just black. It, Luke can't think *he,* it turns and faces him. He takes a step back and the binoculars whack his chest. Suddenly he is aware how close the roof edge is. He drops to his knees, not sure if he is grounding himself or trying to lower his profile for that strange creature on the other roof.

Back on the ground, back inside with the door locked, Luke stands gazing into his second glass of water. What's he going to do? He can't phone anyone. No smartphone was one condition of him staying here on his own. Would anyone believe him anyway? He realises he's shivering and drinks the rest of the water. He finds a sweater and feels a bit better.

He whistles, resisting the urge to think about what he's seen and busies himself setting up the wood stove. He must eat some time. He doesn't need to go outside. In the morning he'll see to the satellite dish.

Then night is upon the cabin and it's fully dark outside. Trying to relax with a book, a murder mystery he'd started at home, he realises he isn't reading. All his senses are attuned to the immediate exterior of the log cabin. He is waiting.

The stove is still warm, though barely, when Luke wakes to cold stiff legs, to a dry throat, to a chill in the air—and to a sibilant sound with a kind of trembling feel to it, an elongated hissing with an undertone of vibration, almost a weird kind of singing. The hair on Luke's arms springs up and a quiver shakes the back of his neck. It's coming from outside.

He turns off the nearer lamp, leaving on the one in the inner room where he'll sleep. That leaves the windows even blacker than they had been in the lamplight. He can't bring himself to approach them, to peer through them. He certainly isn't going outside.

The sound fades, then resumes, a little further away. It strengthens and he realises it sounds like singers conversing. It fades completely.

No point looking outside. The night may be starlit but there's no moon, no other source of light. He flees to bed and hunkers down. In the morning, he's not sure if he's slept.

The rest of his solo time is uneventful. The elderly Randalls turn up the same day his parents and Sophie arrive.

He never tells anyone. The koalas are still in the gum tree.

980 words

PARADIGM SHIFT

The baby care nurse took the tiny baby from its mother, who sighed and raised her hands in a hesitant gesture. They looked together into the baby's face ('This is Harriet,' said the mother) and watched as the baby looked first at the nurse then at her mother, clearly focusing on them.

'She's too little to do that,' the mother said, 'but she's been doing it since she was two weeks old.'

'She is too little to do it,' replied the nurse, 'but she's not the first.'

#

Four years before, the first such baby appeared, the first as far as western nations were concerned. There had been rumours for some time that there was something weird happening in the less developed countries when it came to population growth. It seemed extremely few babies were being born. There was a concomitant and secretive, or at least unacknowledged, leap in sorcery particularly among the villages where tribal custom held sway, where the men ruled.

The occasional American or Canadian or French medic working in primitive places reported strange goings on among the couples having children, but there were no photographs, no video, so it was not news.

When Josie and Kevin McAdam delightedly became a pregnant couple, every moment that could be filmed was recorded for posterity.

Josie and Kevin had been trying for so long to get pregnant that when it happened, they could hardly believe it. They were on the verge of looking into IVF when Josie discovered she was pregnant. That was the last day of January 2135 and she was six weeks along. Josie's mother told her to take it easy, do nothing too strenuous, keep active, eat well, avoid alcohol—all the usual admonitions. Kevin's mother smiled and smiled—their first grandchild!—and piled the young couple with hugely age-inappropriate sets of clothing for both a baby boy and a baby girl.

Josie stayed active and well, as advised. One night when the pregnancy was four months along, as usual Josie was up to the bathroom every couple of hours. Just after 4.00am after one such trip, she woke Kevin, saying, 'My tummy hurts.'

They talked about her discomfort, and she decided it wasn't too bad, might even be that a longer visit to the toilet would be needed (she hadn't had a bowel motion for a couple of days), and tried to go back to sleep.

She had dozed off when she felt something happening and elbowed Kevin awake. He reached for the bedside lamp as Josie lifted the covers to find watery blood between her pyjama-clad legs and on the sheet. She eased the pyjamas off and there, in the blood, was an oval—thing. It was soft and opaque, about 20cm long, but they could see it held a baby, curled in on itself. It was entirely enclosed by a membrane that darkened as they gazed at it. Within minutes it was a hardening dark pink shell, and it pulsed. There was no placental cord and Josie held it to her chest, ignoring the sticky wetness still adhering, her eyes filling. 'We're losing it, aren't we?'

Kevin placed his hand on the shell, the egg, saying, 'It's still alive. Feel the pulse.'

Somehow they simply accepted this was their baby; it came out of Josie, of course it was.

They kept the egg in a warm place; in fact they took turns having it snug against their chests, or their bellies, wherever the cloth folded around it felt most comfortable. Kevin surprised himself by his feelings about it, almost maternal he told Josie one day.

Kevin felt quite justified in his increased emotional connection to the baby when he discovered after the birth that little Emma had a huge increase in microbiota from him, rather than the usual maternal contribution which accompanied a vaginal birth. Caesarean sections allowed for less such microbiota from the mother, but her skin and the hospital surroundings added more, while the father's contribution was usually minimal.

The four grandparents knew and told no one. They were too frightened by the whole thing.

When the baby in the egg was six months old, it was too big for the shell which simply cracked around it.

Within two weeks, baby Emma was responding to their smiles and smiling back.

Baby Emma was the first authenticated in the West but by no means the last. Who could say how many had been born and abandoned elsewhere as monsters?

#

More and more babies were born this way, too early, too aware, and it wasn't long before everyone knew someone who knew someone who'd had an egg baby. Doctors and scientists pondered and talked and conferred, and the babies, more and more, were born from eggnant mothers—a word that crossed readily from animal to human.

The births were almost a 50-50 split, with females slightly in the lead as was the norm in the ordinary population. The babies were small, the prediction being that they would grow no taller than 170 centimetres, the females likely a little shorter. They were intelligent, which pleased the parents. Society at large found it hard: tiny babies, born so oddly, born too soon.

Decades before the first egg baby, total world population reached a peak, then a plateau, and then began to fall. It needed to fall, to settle back to a level that was sustainable, and it had. 12 billion had become nine billion, then six billion and now four billion was in sight. Further falls were inevitable.

Now, pregnancy was lasting four months; mothers barely noticed the condition before they suddenly and painlessly gave birth to a child who completed growing outside the womb and was relating to them two weeks after breaking through the placental shell.

Then one particular peculiarity began to reveal itself which combined with everything else soon had people realising these babies really did belong in the modern world.

These children enjoyed nibbling on plastic—the soft flexible kind of plastic. They sought it out, liking it as a snack. It was this, the reality of humans eating plastic, that convinced scientists that human evolution was taking a mighty detour. It was a paradigm shift that would probably ensure the survival of the human race.

It was going to be interesting to see what else these smaller different humans could do, and be.

1064 words

SOMETHING IN THE LEAVES

Because it was a warm sunny day, Toby's mother was letting him play in the back garden, his favourite place. Surrounded by high fences that Toby didn't notice, the garden was his private wonderland.

There were tall leafy trees and birds that sang, and bushes and shrubs of all kinds. There was plenty of grass too, mostly lawn near the house but long grass as well among the trees and shrubs.

The balls and wooden toys and tricycle on the lawn didn't attract Toby. He turned and waved to his mother who was sitting on the back porch and he took off on the journey. Way down the back he had discovered a bush with pretty red flowers that tasted sweet and juicy and he knew just where to find it.

He fell over twice and grazed his knees but he didn't bother about that. He was distracted once by a bird singing above him and he stood for a while trying to spot it among the leaves. Then he remembered the red flowers and set off again.

The longer grass tickled and scratched his bare legs and he kicked at it happily. He felt in control in this patch. He found the red flowers and picked two, then he wandered away with one in each hand to study the loose bark on one of the trees. He'd pull some of it off when he was ready.

He heard a rustling in the leaves that lay around the tree and he looked about to trace the sound. He'd watched a bird in the leaves once and enjoyed the actions of the perky little creature before it saw him and took fright. Maybe there was another bird he could watch.

Toby's blond hair shone in the dappled sunlight as he moved. The leaves crunched under his bare feet and when he had taken a few steps, he couldn't hear the rustling sound any more.

He leaned against the tree to peek around it, one red flower squashing in his hand. He stood silently, looking carefully through the mat of leaves. He couldn't see a bird anywhere. There wasn't even a little lizard. But then he saw something even better.

A little man, two little men. They were standing back-to-back, looking around fearfully, alert to danger.

Toby said, 'Dolly!' and dropped a flower to pick one of them up. The tiny creature lay kicking in Toby's grip, his breath all but cut off by Toby's enormous thumb across his throat. A strangled sound came from the figure and the tiny man on the ground raised an arm towards Toby. Toby shouted with delight and joy as a kaleidoscope of colours erupted in the air before him. He opened both hands to grab, gurgling with pleasure, the falling figure forgotten.

The pretty colours disappeared suddenly and Toby frowned. He looked for the little moving dollies again and found them among the leaves. They were hard to see because their dark skin and dark clothing blended so well with the autumn cast-offs in which they were waist deep.

Since the pretty colours were gone, Toby would have a dolly again.

He leaned over and picked up the other little man. He had been bending over his companion who was lying among the leaves. Held tightly around his body by Toby's grubby hand, he was brought up to Toby's eye level. Panting, the tiny man opened a miniature hand and held it palm up to Toby.

A miniature silver thing glinted in the sunlight that filtered through the branches high above them, and Toby delicately picked the silver thing from the hand. As he did so, the pretty colours danced before him and Toby laughed aloud.

Clutching the tiny silver ball, he tried to catch the colours with the other hand, dropping the little man on top of his colleague, who had managed to stand. Together they crawled away through the leaves, trying to be quiet, to remain unnoticed.

Toby was too engrossed with the colours to be aware of them. He must show Mummy. With the thought, his mother was there in front of him, where the pretty colours had been.

Waving his arms and shouting to her incoherently, he told her about the pretty colours. As he talked about them they returned in all their splendour. Delighted, he watched them until he remembered his mother. Again she was there, smiling, but the colours were gone.

He looked around for them, and there they were, but his mother was gone. Frustrated, Toby began walking towards the house. He would get Daddy. Daddy would stay and look at the colours with him. At once his Daddy was in front of him and Toby began talking about the colours to him. Again the colours returned, but his Daddy was gone.

Hot tears sprang easily into his eyes. The colours went away and his Daddy went away. He wanted Mummy. His mother came, standing in front of him with her arms open. Soothed by her appearance again he started to talk about the colours. They were there suddenly but his mother vanished.

It was too much. Roaring his outrage, Toby turned for the house, silver ball clutched in his fist and tears streaming down his face.

His mother reached him at the end of the lawn and picked him up. His crying turned to hiccupping sobs and he tried to tell her, again, about the dollies in the leaves and the pretty colours that kept on coming and going.

As he pictured them and tried to talk about them, first the little men and then the colours appeared before him. Quite unable to understand his babble, Toby's mother soothed him and opened his clenched fist. She'd have to get rid of that. A ball bearing, a new one by the look of it, was too easy for a toddler to swallow.

With the silver ball gone from his grasp, Toby could no longer see either the colours or the dollies. He took a breath, preliminary to a fresh spate of tears. Then he paused. Over his mother's shoulder he could see a tennis ball sized object with sparkling lights around its middle skimming along the grass behind her.

He fell silent, his thumb in his mouth and watched with interest as it hovered uncertainly above the paving stones near the back door. He took his thumb from his mouth to point a finger at it, telling his mother to look. It rose slowly and just as it disappeared beyond the guttering above the kitchen, she turned with a sigh to see what he was getting excited about.

1110 words

THE DOOR OPENS

'It's really mysterious. Mysterious and fascinating.'

'I wish I could see it.'

'I wish you could, too,' Leo's mother told him. She was cutting up onions, sniffing. 'There are six UFOs in different parts of the world. Obviously UFOs. Saucer shaped, huge, silvery, standing flat on the ground. They landed almost simultaneously and since then, nothing.'

Leo knew all this. There had been an uproar when the flying saucer landed on the field outside their town. It just sat there, though the ramp had slid down to the ground soon after it landed. No one came out; there was no reaction to armed soldiers or helicopters. There was no activity that anyone could see.

Leo trailed his fingers over a page in his Braille book. 'And one is right on the edge of our town. Dad said he might take me in. If our UFO continues to do nothing, he might get permission for me to touch it.'

Washing her hands, his mother watched with understanding as Leo fingered the texture of the place mat under his book, ran his fingers along the edge of the wooden table then rested them again on his book.

'I'll leave you to your reading,' she said, and as she turned back to the vegetables, the phone rang.

Leo sat up straighter as he listened. Dad was still at work by the sound of it, not coming home any time soon. He listened intently, knowing when his mother turned to look at him. Her skirt or pants whispered against the kitchen bench and her voice came more directly towards him.

'That's amazing! What does it mean?' She paused to listen. Then, 'Yes, I'm sure he'll want to. I'll turn off the stove and put the food away then we'll come in … okay, I'll tell him then we'll come in.'

'What? What is it? What was amazing? Are we going into Dad's work, to the UFO?' She was taking her time getting to him.

She gently pushed him down on his seat and pulled a chair closer. 'This is what your dad says. He needs you to go in.'

'*Needs* to?' A frisson, a shiver, travelled up Leo's spine, tingled the back of his neck. 'He needs me?'

'Hmm. Apparently something strange is going on. Your dad says Jason Milton was with his dad today. His mum's not well, and Toby took him to work for the day.'

Leo knew little Jason well. Both being blind was a bond that worked even though there were ten years between them. The toddler was a ball of energy, and like Leo, had been born blind. Their families barbecued together in the summer.

The two fathers worked together at the small-town offshoot of NASA, operating huge radar dishes and watching the skies. Jason had long accepted that he would never see what his dad regularly saw: planets and comets and amazing sights like the rings around Saturn.

'What else, Mum?'

'Apparently,' Will could feel the shrug in his mother's voice, 'when he was near the UFO today, he said someone came out.'

'Who said? Do you mean Jason?'

'Yep. Jason. Blind Jason.'

They sat silently for a moment. 'And no one else, uh, saw this?' Leo was frowning.

'I'll tell you what your dad said. Because there'd been no activity other than the ramp coming down, Jason's dad is allowed to take him towards the ramp. He'll be allowed to step on it, and then off. He wants to touch the UFO, but only the ramp today. Then the door at the top of the ramp opens and according to Jason, someone comes out.'

Will took a deep breath and turned his head to follow his mother as she began clearing the dinner preparations away. 'No one knows what he's talking about,' his mother continued, 'but the temperature drops in the immediate vicinity and Jason starts talking to invisible beings.'

'He told his dad, and your dad, that he can see them. Jason wants you to come and see them. Jason's still blind but he can see these people. He says they smile a lot.'

#

'Can you see them?'

Leo nodded in response to his dad's question. He might be blind, but just like Jason, he could see the aliens. Leo led his father by the hand towards the silvery saucer-shaped craft. Behind them, Jason was whinging and complaining, his voice penetrating. 'I want to go too, I want to go too.'

Leo said quietly to his dad, 'Jason's too little to talk to them,' and squeezed the hand holding his. Leo could feel his dad turn briefly. He must have glanced back at the small crowd standing behind noisy Jason.

His dad said, 'There's just the ramp from the open door. If I squint,' he added, 'I can just make out a kind of shimmer, two of them.'

'That's the aliens, Dad. I can see them.'

Normal human vision can only see visible light so the scientists couldn't see the aliens, who must consist of some kind of electromagnetic radiation. That's what Leo's dad figured. Now, here he was, walking towards an alien spacecraft where aliens waited for him. Right now, Leo could make out their faces and Jason was right. He had said the aliens smiled.

One of them gestured, indicating Leo should come ahead on his own and Leo told his dad, who let him go—it was only a couple of metres—and Leo walked up the ramp. They conversed for a time, Leo shaking his head a couple of times, raising his shoulders and arms in a pleading manner. Cameras were whirring.

Slowly, Leo turned away from the aliens and walked down the ramp. 'We have to get back under cover, Dad,' he said. 'They're leaving. It's dangerous to be this close when it takes off.'

'What did they say?'

Leo shook his head sadly. 'I'll tell you inside.' Behind them, the ramp was drawing back into the spacecraft. A barely-sensed vibration that built to a crescendo and then faded meant the craft was gone.

Cameras on him, Leo faced the small crowd. 'They're leaving,' he said, 'and never coming back again. They've been here many times before but never again. They usually hide their ship, cloak it or whatever, but it doesn't matter this time, they said. This is their final collecting expedition.'

Questions were thrown at him, and Leo held up a hand. 'Usually they try not to be seen, but this last time it didn't matter. They don't want to talk to anyone else. They were surprised when Jason saw them.'

Someone else asked, 'Why were they here?'

Leo took a deep breath. 'For years they've collected birds and insects and seeds; flowers, trees, vegetables, all kinds of seeds. They've made a point of saving birds because most planets don't have them, though some do.'

'Why were they here now?' one of his dad's colleagues asked Leo.

'Earth's creatures and plants are unique in the universe and with Earth in its dreadful condition, they've been collecting like mad.'

His shoulders drooped and his dad squeezed his shoulder. 'Take me home, please, Dad.'

Someone shouted at him, 'What did they want this time? This last time?'

Leo turned and told them. 'They came for the butterflies.'

1217 words

THE SECRET IN THE PINE FOREST

I've never told anyone about this before and I don't expect you to believe it. But it happened.

My sister Susie and I always enjoyed playing with our cousins, the Laceys, in the school holidays. Their last name was actually Lacefield and they were twins. Susie and I didn't see much of them during school time. They went to a different school, a posh one where they got in trouble if their socks slipped down around their ankles. Our school was pretty happy if we turned up at all. Luckily, Susie and I never got into strife at school so our parents didn't go to our school much. I don't remember them ever going when I think about it.

The twins, Arabella and Zaria, A and Z, pretty cool we thought as ten-year-olds—they were kept really busy all term. Their mum, our mum's sister, owned a chain of hair salons, she was a businesswoman. Their dad was something high in the education department, so the girls were required to show respect for his position by never ever getting into trouble, by always achieving high marks in everything, by volunteering, to suck up to teachers whenever needed. They had dance lessons and music lessons and hockey. They were never allowed to be themselves.

Except for a few days in the holidays. After going to camp and visiting relatives and buying new clothes for the new term, none of which we could afford, there were two days at the end of the holidays when Aunty Karen and Uncle Don went away and Bella and Zaria spent two nights and the days with us.

Mum told us once that the Laceys thought it was good for their girls to know their cousins as they'd be going away to boarding school for all their high school years. Susie and I were the two youngest of five. Two brothers and a sister with a gap of five years to me and then only a year and a half to Susie. The twins fitted between us in age. Our brothers were all grown up and we hardly saw them, and our sister was at high school and we hardly saw her either.

Zaria told me once that her dad respected our dad. Our dad was a lawyer who 'fought for the downtrodden'—that's what he said. Mum was at home all the time and famous in our street for her biscuits and cakes. Mm, nothing better than coming up our street on a cold afternoon after the bus dropped us off to smell Mum's cooking three houses away. I reckon Aunty Karen respected that, 'cause she couldn't cook for quids.

Anyway, now that you know that, let me tell you about the time Bella and I had an experience in our pine forest we could never tell anyone about.

It wasn't really a pine forest. At the end of our cul-de-sac was an undeveloped piece of land with about six pine trees. I think there was a right of way or an underground culvert or something legal that meant it was left to itself. Mum could see it from our gate, so she didn't mind us going there in a group. It was great for playing in and we often went there. We spent one time together making a little garden. It was only about a metre square—we ran out of puff digging the soil—and we pinched bits of plants from our garden and we politely asked at a few other houses in the street and were given plants.

During school term Susie and I watered it now and then but mostly we forgot. So it was a real surprise to find a lovely little garden growing the next time we were all together. Full of weeds but they looked like they belonged, so we left them alone.

We all brought tiny things from home—miniature furniture, little containers we turned upside down and partly hid under the flowers. The only flower name I knew was zinnia, and a couple of them stood tall like colourful giant umbrellas in the mini garden.

We used to lie on our bellies and arrange little troll dolls with brightly coloured hair among the greenery. Other tiny toys were laid about here and there. They had great adventures and I used some of the stories in my school compositions. My English teacher thought I was really clever but the stories really came from the four of us.

One of the tiny dolls we played with was a beautiful fairy of Bella's. She was about 4cm high with golden curls and a gorgeous light and dark blue ballerina gown and silver slippers. Bella never left her there overnight like we did with all the others. We felt they were pretty safe as no one ever lingered in our pine forest.

Well, one day the fairy was left behind. She was sitting back against a velvet lounge (actually a bit of velvet from my older sister's sewing box) and was resting her silver slippers on an empty matchbox. She wasn't touching the ground.

A storm broke suddenly and we sped back to our place. When the storm had passed it was getting dark, and Bella suddenly remembered her fairy. Mum gave her and me permission to go back to the pine forest together to fetch her. We assured Mum we knew exactly where she was. All the same she stood out on the path near our letterbox to watch us go down the street.

It was pretty wet underfoot and Bella was worried that the fairy doll might have been damaged by the rain. I was expecting to see her looking bedraggled, maybe even dirty from rain-splashed soil.

We could see Mum behind us when we looked but it was still a bit creepy walking into the darkening pine forest, then the moon began to break through the clouds and it was quite pretty, the moonlight splashing a pale glimmer through the trees. The ground was not only wet, it was noisy with the pine needles crunching under our feet, so Bella and I began to tiptoe to keep our footsteps quiet. I don't know why, we just did. We held hands to make each other steadier.

When we reached the little garden we both hunkered down and looked among the tiny things. The moonlight lit up the scene and Bella squeezed my hand, quite hard. I glanced at her, then at where she was looking. I started squeezing back and held my breath.

The light blue of the fairy doll's ballerina gown glowed in the moonlight and the dark blue parts contrasted with her skin-coloured arms and legs. Her arms were being held by two tiny creatures that had wings fluttering furiously to help them stay upright as they lowered the fairy doll into her position against the velvet. It looked as though it might have been caught in the rain, dappled with dark spots all over. The little people were wearing floaty gowns of some kind, the colour of moonlight. I think one had a headband of really tiny flowers. I remember hints of yellow and purple.

The two fairies held hands, just like Bella and me, and hovered in front of the little fairy doll. I wondered what they could be thinking. Their backs were to us and I was hoping they'd show us their faces but all at once one turned her head a little and in a blink they were gone. She must have seen us.

Bella and I both sighed a deep long-held-in breath. We looked at each other and let go our hands. She reached over for the fairy doll but hesitated, her hand quivering. She picked her up.

'I'd love to leave it for them,' she said to me quietly, 'but Mum would kill me. Aunty Dee gave it to me.' She looked all around and said in a louder voice, 'I'd love to leave it here but I can't. I'm sorry.'

We played in the pine forest with Susie and Zaria only a few more times before life sent us in different directions.

We never told anyone. We never talked about it together. We never called the fairy doll *she* again.

1381 words

MAD MELPI

Sama and Altha lay on their backs on the pale pink grass watching the moon rise above the western horizon. High above them the minor sun cast its pale glow. A light breeze gently lifted their outer tendrils but their underfur stayed warm. Both girls began to scratch idly at an abdomen crease where their tendrils tickled.

Altha turned her head to stare at her friend. 'Melpi wants you to steal something from that weird place, the one that's full of junk and trash and litter from the seven worlds? But why?'

'It's a challenge.' Sama sighed. 'You know what they're like when they get together, these stupid spoiled females, so rich they don't need to lift a finger, and idle as can be. Mad Melpi—' Altha chuckled at the epithet— 'has accepted a challenge from Rosta.' Sama shook her head in despair.

'What's the challenge?'

'Rosta made one of her slaves, Mita, steal something from the store even though the owner was watching. Just for fun, Rosta said, but not much fun for Mita. So now Melpi simply must do the same, only bigger and better. Rosta's girl stole an old Earth thing, a little flat metal thing full of holes. The heavens only know what it's for. I have to steal something bigger than *this—'* Sama held her hands body width apart, her furry ringlets wafting with the breeze.

'Well, we'd better go and see what we can find.' Altha stood decisively.

The writing on the store appeared to be in old Earth language.

Inside, Sama moved up to the person behind the counter. His eyes were alert even though he yawned in her face as she neared him.

Sama said, 'What does the name of your store mean? How do you pronounce it?'

'I don't know, and I don't say it at all. How could I know how humans talk? All the signs in here are in the original languages of their worlds. It shows their authenticity. I don't have to read them or speak them.'

Shrugging off his disdain, the girls wandered through the aisles of piled-up things that littered every flat surface. They picked up all kinds of strange items. They turned over odd shapes, they lifted small objects and studied them, and they shook and listened to outlandish items that they simply could not understand.

Altha went one way and Sama the other and shortly Sama heard Altha hissing, beckoning to her through a gap. 'Look,' Altha said. 'This is much bigger than Rosta's thing, isn't it?'

'Yes! And it's beautiful too.'

A piece of material was suspended by a couple of pegs above a table. It appeared to be perfectly square, each side three times the width of Sama's body. Feeling an edge, Sama immediately fell in love with it. It was so smooth, so cool to the touch, so colourful. It showed a pleasing scene in many colours. It looked like flat blue water—blue! —with yellow soil and a number of what she knew to be humans lying or walking on the yellow soil. Some were actually in the blue water, if that's what it was. Vibrant colourful little roofs were dotted here and there. Its sign named it Silk Scarf.

'I know how you can steal this, Sama,' Altha said confidently

After hearing her friend's idea, Sama went to the owner. 'My friend and I have to go in and out a few times to talk to our mistresses. Is that all right?'

As Sama left, the owner went on a tour of inspection. The other slave was handling some small pretty items of jewellery marked Beads Lockets Trinkets. She smiled at him. 'My friend will be back soon.' He grunted, not notice that Silk Scarf, still suspended from its pegs, had been folded in half.

Sama returned with credits from her mistress. Just a few, to buy something, anything. When Altha went out the owner toured again. This time Silk Scarf was a quarter its original size and lying on the table below the pegs. Altha remained when Sama left once more, having told the owner that her mistress couldn't make up her mind about a purchase. He shrugged. This time he didn't bother to check on the other slave.

By the time each of them had been outside and in once more, Silk Scarf was a thick lump not much bigger than Sama's hand. She tucked it into the second of her abdomen folds and stood behind Altha as she handed over the credits for a small bag filled with Beads Lockets Trinkets. Altha thought Sama would probably end up with them—though you never knew with Melpi. She'd maybe want to adorn her own body with the pretty Earth things though she'd have to coil her fur to attach each one. Ouch!

When Sama gave her the oh-so-tiny Silk Scarf, Melpi erupted. 'It's too small, you stupid girl!' Screeching incoherently, Melpi tried to slap Sama's face but she swayed back beyond Melpi's reach. Then, leaning in, Sama plucked the item from Melpi's hand. Holding just one corner, Sama swung Silk Scarf up and down and up again until it billowed out between them, soft and colourful and beautiful and big.

Now Melpi was screeching again, this time with glee.

Melpi became generous for a time and life for Sama was easier than it had been. Melpi trusted her more and actually sought her opinion about household matters. Sama might be a slave but life wasn't too bad. Until, some time later, Sama was standing outside her home, her mistress's home, fuming, frowning, puzzled.

Where on Earth could she go? Now that would be funny if she weren't so downhearted. Earth was exactly where she needed to go, but it just wasn't possible. Where should she try? Maybe someone at the old museum would have some idea. But first she'd go back to the Silk Scarf store, the one she and Altha had robbed for Melpi. There'd been no repercussions as far as Sama knew and it was a store that had all kinds of exotic items.

Walking tall, pretending confidence, Sama entered the store and immediately encountered the eyes of the same rather unwelcoming person behind the counter. There was no particular reaction from him, just his usual suspicious stare. It didn't appear that he remembered her. Maybe he'd never noticed Silk Scarf was gone. Maybe Melpi had fixed it somehow.

Sama had no real hope that the store would have what she wanted, but she had to try. At least the staff might have a suggestion about where to search.

'Tights? Ah, tights. Yes, I do know what they are. In fact I was looking at a picture of them just this morning. I like to keep up with these alien outlandish things. Luckily this book has translations. Tights. . . tights. . . women's. . . Earth..'

He reached into a hidden nook behind the counter to bring out a colourful book of some sort and leafed through it.

'Look. Finely made leg coverings, mostly worn by women on old Earth. Goodness knows what for! Certainly not for warmth by the look of them.'

Averting her eyes from the alien figures in their alien wrappings, Sama enquired about the possibility of purchasing some, but the response was a laugh. One hand holding the book open, while the fingers on his other hand stretched to complete various tasks, the unattractive creature stared at Sama. One finger was rootling inside an ear, another scratching an irritation on his neck and the third pointing at her in derision.

'Some things from old Earth we've kept, my dear, but hardly items of clothing. Communications systems, interstellar travel, names, some everyday household goods, but not clothing.'

He dismissed her with a languid wave, still laughing at the idea.

Sama stood in despair outside the store. Melpi did not like to be thwarted. Melpi would kill her if she didn't produce "tights". She felt wretched. How dreadful to belong to a mistress who had nothing better to do than to lie about all day thinking up outrageous outfits to wear to the all-night parties she loved. And thinking up bizarre ways to compete with her equally idle friends.

And now she wanted "tights". She'd heard about them from someone; she couldn't say what they were, what they looked like or on what part of the body they belonged—but she wanted them.

Sama's feet dragged as she went on down the street. Where else should she try to find the exotic piece of clothing? Her very life could be forfeit if she failed—she might have to stow away on a ship lifting off planet. Her friend Altha had talked about doing that last year. She'd thought she might have to vanish when her mistress expected her to find some gaudy thing or other from old Earth. What was it called, a hangle or fangle. No that wasn't it —a bangle!

Thank goodness she'd recalled that worrying time because now Sama remembered too that Altha didn't have to leave and she didn't get killed either. She managed to produce the wangle, bangle, whatever it was. In fact, it was probably seeing the thing on Altha's mistress that prompted Melpi's current hankering. Now, where would she find Altha?

The next day, following Altha's advice, Sama entered a little shop tucked away in an inconspicuous alley off the main thoroughfare. Altha had said it was a specialist weaving shop, that it was staffed by weird types from some really distant planet, and that they could produce anything in the way of body coverings. And so it proved to be.

Trying to avoid looking into the multifaceted eyes—hard to do when they were a hypnotising rainbow of flickering colour—Sama described the tights as best she could. She'd caught only a glimpse of them in the other store's book, but she remembered where on the body they should be worn.

Now, walking blithely down the same alley with her purse lightened by an exorbitant number of Melpi's credits, Sama was content. With luck Melpi would give her some time off. She knew Melpi would just love the pale golden tights, the material woven so delicately that one could see right through it.

Her mistress need never know that originally tights had only two legs.

1733 words

SUCCESSFUL VISIT

The ship's light-deflecting forcefield made it virtually invisible in dim light, especially in an unsuspecting environment. Its navigator followed normal precautions however and landed it in the darkest part of the aerodrome, two kilometres from the terminal building.

The expedition member chosen for this particular foray had no difficulty reaching the lighted area close to the building, his natural glow blending with the yellow light that suffused the area.

He flowed under an aircraft, a small version of the primitive flying machines on this planet, and immediately had a stroke of luck. A tall grey-haired male in dark blue was striding towards the aircraft and it was a simple matter for the alien to enter the man's body, turn it around and start it walking back to the building. He passed through an electrically operated door into a brightly lit corridor. There were doors in both walls, some closed, some open. The alien heard voices, which could have been speaking to the man he was in, but he ignored them. He had to get among a group of humans quickly to give him a wider choice for a temporary host and ultimately an appropriate specimen.

He walked the tall body into a very large room, also brightly lit. There were plenty of humans. Some were sitting, others standing singly and in groups, in long rows in front of counters, most with baggage near them. It was perfect.

He felt something clutch at the clothing on his host's arm. A hand had grabbed at him, and a voice was speaking urgently, directly at him. "Captain, Captain." He shook the hand off, thinking rapidly. He needed to be in a stationary body for a time to work out just what to do. Near him a fat female was sitting alone, her legs stretched out before her as though she were exhausted.

Abruptly leaving the tall man and entering the fat woman, the alien watched with interest as the tall man recovered his senses. It was a woman with blonde hair who had clutched at him and she was looking up into the tall man's face with a worried expression. The alien gazed at the blonde hair with interest. It was not a natural body colour in his home world.

The tall man said clearly, 'What am I doing in here? I was just going on board. God, am I going crazy?'

The humans often mentioned God, though usually they said, 'Oh my God!', the alien observed.

The woman's voice was lowered as she led him away. 'It's all right. Don't worry about it."

They disappeared through a doorway and the alien brought his attention back to his surroundings. He was sitting, or his female host was sitting, in a comfortable seat with a good view of all the humans. The alien noted the woman who had taken the tall man away now walking past with another man, shorter than the first and with black hair, but also dressed in dark blue. They went into the corridor, murmuring together and vanished from sight. The new man must be taking the tall man's place.

There was a lesson here, the alien realised. His choice of a specimen must be someone who was not important, just an ordinary man who would not be missed. He must not choose someone in the dark blue clothing. The only requirement was that it must be a man. The spaceship had on board the sleeping bodies of five women and four men and he had to choose a fifth man.

He gazed at all the men he could see, in no hurry. He had an hour, local time, before he had to deliver the specimen to his ship, if possible with a small easily carried artefact in common use. Most of the humans had nothing with them when they were collected and local objects were wanted too. One of the many cases he could see would be ideal.

Sharp pain low in the back suddenly struck the female body, making the alien wince. He raised the clamp on the woman's mind sufficiently for her to sit herself upright and place a hand to the small of her back, where she rubbed the painful area vigorously. The alien could feel improvement at once but the woman's mind began straining against his hold and he imposed the curb on her.

Suddenly he was distracted by sensation within the woman's abdomen. Something was moving inside the body! He eased the control on the female's mind and discovered the truth. This female was actually bearing within her a human creature waiting to be born! He had been told about this weird method of reproduction but hadn't really understood. He flinched as the movements strengthened and wondered at the delight he could sense, deep in the woman's mind. How disgusting to experience this personally though his superiors would be interested. For now he must get out of this situation.

He glanced around rapidly. Luck must be with him still, for passing in front of him was the perfect specimen, and he was carrying in his hand one of the rectangular containers so many of the humans had with them.

Immediately the alien quit the female body and took over the man. This body was shorter than the other man he had possessed but appeared to be a fit and healthy specimen, dressed in what the alien judged to be common clothing. He seemed to be a very ordinary male human.

They sat some seats away from the pregnant woman who was looking around in a puzzled manner. She probably thought she had been sleeping. The alien had been told some humans retained a vestige of memory of the occupying mind but most thought they had been sleeping and dreaming. He lifted the artefact from the floor and placed it on his lap. He did not want to lose it. It was quite heavy for its size and he wondered idly what was in it. It had metal clasps that clearly allowed it to open. That was not his concern. He had only to get it and its owner safely to the ship.

He still had time to spare so he sat back, nursing the case. He watched the busy humans at their affairs and almost retreated into sleep, lulled as he was by the constant flow of people before him. Discomfort in his lower abdomen made itself felt and he was startled. Not again! He waited a moment to see if it would disappear but it was intensifying. Surely this male body could not have a growing creature inside it, unless the information he had received about humans was wrong.

Perhaps the body had some disease. He cautiously lifted the restraint on the man's mind and with relief discovered a need to pass fluid. He had been warned of such bodily functions so he got the man to his feet and allowed him to lead the way. Unfortunately the man's thoughts became chaotic with fear, not an unusual reaction with human specimens. Oddly the fear seemed to be connected to the suitcase in the man's hand. The alien resisted the man's strong urge to hide the artefact, the 'case' or 'bag', and forced him to concentrate on the increasing discomfort within. The human, rigid with the effort to wrest control of himself back from whatever had him in its grip, walked stiffly to a doorway with writing on it, entered the room inside and eventually did what had to be done.

There was a struggle between them at first for the alien did not want to release the case, but the human clearly needed both hands for his clothing and to pass his fluid from his body. This would be interesting to report. Immediately he was finished the man tried to turn away and run but the alien compelled him to turn back to the case and pick it up. Then the alien took total control and the human subsided.

Best to go straight to the ship. This human was troublesome. A plump balding man was sitting in the seat they had left and he leapt to his feet in front of the alien's human.

"What's the matter with you? They'll be through here in twenty-five minutes. Get rid of it!"

The alien felt the man's features shift in a grimace as he lifted control a little from his mind. "I can't get rid of it. Something, somebody, I don't know what, something won't let me."

"What are you talking about, you fool? Here, give it to me."

The plump stranger went to snatch the case away so the alien left his host abruptly, leaving the man staggering. He entered the other man's mind and blasted it. He fell heavily to the floor as the alien re-entered his host and set the body walking away, case firmly held. He heard a commotion behind him as he forced the human to walk quickly down the corridor to the exit.

No one took any notice as they left the building. In front of them was another aircraft while in the distance a craft was just taking to the air. Once in the shadows he searched for power lines, any would do, and found them high on a wall. He concentrated on them and flames appeared. Lights went out all over the area and tumult broke out.

In his pleasure at his success, the alien allowed his restraint on the human's mind to slip a little but the resulting agitation made him reimpose it at once. In the darkness it was easy if tiring on the human's body to walk the two kilometres to the landing site, as the case seemed to become heavier and heavier.

Then they were on board and the ship was lifting away. His human host had his mind to himself for a brief period, but the aliens took no notice at all of his fearful expression as he watched his case being passed from one creature to another. It was a common expression on the faces of human specimens before they were made to sleep.

The security unit detailed to the British Prime Minister congratulated themselves on their good work as the ministerial plane took off from the small Irish airport. They never heard about the puzzling and unexplained flare of light in the night sky minutes before the departure.

1738 words

FUTURE ECHOES

'Where are we anyway?' demanded Trudy as her dad drove away. She leaned over the rail that kept pedestrians on the footpath. The entrance to the supermarket was a few metres to our left and the taxi rank to our right. A half dozen shopping trolleys made a straight line against the wall behind us, a couple of stragglers looking as though they couldn't make up their minds whether to join the queue.

'Aunty Jane's shopping centre,' I replied.

'I think I've been here before,' Trudy said, looking around. We had all been here before, more than once, but the view was just a road with a car park and a street with cars speeding by, and along from us two taxis waiting. We waited, we window shopped, Trudy and Jennifer squabbled half-heartedly, and we waited. All at once Jane and her two sons were there in their van.

Climbing into the van, Trudy commented, 'You two do look alike,' to my sister Jane and me. Josh and Matthew made room for the two girls, laughing and joking with them. My sister grinned at me. 'She always says that.' She started the vehicle and glanced over her shoulder at the traffic. 'And I don't think we do, anyhow.'

'I haven't said it before,' protested Trudy, 'have I, Mum?'

I said, 'It doesn't matter if you have. You're entitled to your opinion, and so is Aunty Jane.' Jennifer's voice, with Josh and Matthew's, chimed in with mine on the last few words. I was startled. They were all grinning at each other when I glanced back at them.

'You do say that sort of thing a lot, Mum,' Jennifer said to me.

'Reminds me of Mum,' I said to Jane, adjusting the belt and settling into the seat.

'Mm,' she replied. 'I do it too. Funny how parental patterns linger on.' We both laughed. We'd talked about this before.

We were a motley lot—me, totally grey, quite young may I add, my sister Jane dark and glossy, Matthew and Josh almost black, and my two daughters both reddish brown like their dad.

Jane and I chatted while the cousins teased each other and remembered past glories of holidays in the bush. Today was just a day trip to Jane's home thirty kilometres from the city. It was 15 acres of largely untouched bush and the girls loved visiting. The cleared land near the house was lovingly tended by Jane, with jacarandas and poincianas alternating throughout the year in displays we couldn't have on our suburban block. Jane's husband ran an increasingly busy interstate trucking business and we wouldn't see him today.

Jane said, 'Have to detour, I'm afraid. Parts to pick up for one or other of the trucks. Matthew's got the details.'

'That's okay. We're spending the day with you all wherever you go.'

'We do want to climb some trees before we go home.' That was Jennifer, my tomboy older girl and at 12 as tall as me. Tallest of the group of cousins.

Matthew, Jane's older boy, said, 'Yeah, we'll climb trees. It won't take long to get these parts.'

'Good,' said his mother. 'What's it called again, Matthew? I can never remember.'

'I can't remember either.' I could hear Matthew's frown in his voice. 'Funny name. Funny place. But I know where to go.' He was distracted by giggles nearby.

'Here.' Jane scrabbled near my feet for a plastic bag. 'Peaches.'

'Ooh, goody.' The bag disappeared behind us. 'And remember,' Jane began, '... tissues in the box behind the driver's seat...' came the chorus. Jane's peaches were famous in the family. Sweet and juicy from well-tended trees.

We soon drove off the main road at Matthew's direction. An enormous warehouse spread out ahead of us low and long as we drove downhill towards it. 'Gee, it's big,' one of my girls said from behind us.

'I don't remember seeing this place before,' I commented, but no one seemed to hear me. I turned to look for a name but the van jolted over a cattle grid filling the space across a gateway and Matthew said, 'In here, to the right, Mum.' There was parking space off to one side, but clearly vehicles were meant to drive into the laneways built into the huge building.

Dark and gloomy caverns loomed ahead. We passed lighted areas with cars pulled up in front of them then plunged back into the dim wide passage. Matthew's hands rustled the paper with his father's instructions. 'Fifth on the left.' Jane parked the van and everyone got out, stretching and yawning. We hadn't been driving that long, I thought, but I was yawning too.

Inside was a long narrow counter with old-fashioned shelves on the walls behind. The shelves were right-angled to the counter and disappeared into the distance. Busy salesmen pattered around. Busy, busy. All men, I noticed for some reason. All men. Very quiet and very busy. Hardly any sounds at all. The children found a drink machine in a corner, brought one each for Jane and me. Matthew and Jane ordered their part and it came surprisingly quickly.

Back at the van, I looked up at Jennifer for a moment as she reached up to Matthew's shoulder to hitch herself into the back of the van. 'Up you go, shorty,' he said. Something's odd, I thought briefly, and turned to Jane. She held out the key. 'Here, you drive for a bit.'

Behind the wheel, I flexed my fingers and inserted the key. The wheel felt strange. For an instant I caught a glimpse of wrongness then my feet found their places and I drove off.

'Good to have a break from driving,' Jane said. I glanced at her, smiling. She was looking in the mirror behind the sun visor. 'Have to pick up my hair colour soon. There's just too much grey showing.'

I laughed. 'You get used to it.' We do look alike, I thought. A vague memory stirred: a little girl had once said something like that. Jane grimaced and sighed, rubbing a hip. 'You too?' I asked. 'Old age creeping up on both of us.'

Jane and I began a session of remember this, and what about so and so. The children were talking quietly, boyfriends, dates, university. Matthew's deep voice intoned, 'Next left.'

I pulled in and we all left the van. The young people strolled into the light and I marvelled at their youth and beauty, their straightness and their strength.

'Such a long drive, Mum,' Jennifer said beside me. 'Let one of us take over for a while. Josh needs the practice and it's pretty safe in these straight lanes.'

I looked into her calm mature face and wondered that such a fine person had come from me. She stayed with me while the part was bought. Back in the van, Josh called back to us, 'One more stop, Mum?' His voice was a mellow baritone.

'Yes, dear,' Jane said from beside me. Her voice quavered just a fraction and I turned, a trifle painfully, to look at her. The children had placed a rug across her lap and her wrinkled hands rested on it. I glanced at my own hands and they were twins of hers. I had a rug too.

Trudy leaned over from the front, beside Josh. 'Everything okay, Mum?' Her auburn hair seemed darker than I remembered with a few streaks of grey. Tiny crows' feet marred her fine skin. I looked past her to my older girl as I answered, 'Of course, everything's fine.' My Jennifer was a middle-aged woman, my little Trudy nearly so. I looked at my hands. Well, the girls would be middle aged, you silly goat.

My hands. I'd always looked after them and now they were so, so old.

Matthew's bulk filled the van as he loomed over us all, directing his brother from the rear. His paunch responded to gravity as he steadied himself with spotted hands on the back of the seat. 'Over there, on the right. Okay, everyone out for the last time.'

My walking stick was a blessing as I trailed the others into the light. 'Last part, thank goodness.' That was Jane, barely audible up ahead. Bloody old age.

My faltering step firmed up on the way back to the van, and Jane's voice was stronger, fuller. 'I'll drive now.'

'You sure, Mum?' Josh relinquished the keys. 'Oh yes,' she replied, and opened the driver's door with a flourish.

'Put this somewhere, will you?' I handed the walking stick into the back of the van and someone took it. It seemed to leap out of my hand.

'Funny place,' I remarked to Jane, beside her in the front. She nodded, eyes ahead and blinking a little.

'Turn right here, Mum.' Matthew was close behind us, kneeling on the van floor. His eyes were level with mine. Why did that surprise me?

'You'll get into trouble if a policeman sees you, Matthew.' He grinned at me and returned to his seat.

'Mum, why don't you learn to drive?' Trudy asked, her voice the clear high sound of a little girl's. Jane suddenly shook herself and I shivered. 'Someone walking on our graves,' she said. We glanced at each other. 'Dad,' we said together and smiled. Our father used to say that.

'I've been thinking about learning to drive,' I answered Trudy. 'I think I'd enjoy it.'

A giggle broke out behind us, then a scuffle. 'Now kids, quieten down. You'll distract the driver.'

'Here.' Jane scrabbled around near my feet and lifted a plastic bag to the seat between us. 'I brought some peaches for you to take home. Save one at least for your Dad. Tissues...'

'...in the box behind the driver's seat,' they all sang.

'I'm starting to feel I'm a bit predictable,' Jane said to me. Then to the children, 'I hope you've all had a good day.'

'It was great, thanks, Aunty Jane. Don't ever cut down those trees, will you?'

She laughed. 'I wouldn't dare. I have to keep them for your children.'

Josh giggled. 'I heard someone say the other day, "live fast, die young, and leave a good-looking corpse". I might do that.'

Jennifer squealed, 'That's awful!'

Oh no, you won't, I thought, and wondered at how sure I felt. To Jane I said, 'Thanks for lunch and for the company. It was lovely, as usual.'

'Here's Uncle Rick waiting,' Josh said. 'See you in a few weeks, girlie cousins.'

'See you, boyey cousins,' Jennifer and Trudy called together. They leaned over between the front seats to kiss Jane. 'Bye, bye, Aunty Jane ... thanks.'

They ran for the car but I lingered at Jane's door. 'What was that place we went to this morning, for the spare parts?'

A frown marred Jane's smooth forehead. 'Parts? I can't remember. Isn't that silly?'

A tremor ran through me. 'I can't remember either.'

Matthew said, 'I remember how to get there but I can never remember what it's called.'

Josh said in a quiet voice, 'I really don't like going there.'

Then my girls were yelling to their cousins and they were yelling back. My husband was wincing at the noise as I reached the car.

On the drive home, for some reason I kept looking at my hands.

1895 words

THE OLD LION

Al and I had been to Africa three or four times. I couldn't remember. We'd never thought of big game hunting since I'd never wanted to, and Al couldn't understand killing for sport. A photographic safari, different story. We were both enjoying it.

I lay in my fancy cabin, dozing. The Land Rover ride today had irritated both my hips, and my backside felt the lack of flesh. I remembered a time when I wished for a skinnier rump—but that was long ago.

Someone walked past on the verandah and its wooden floor squeaked. It reminded me of being on the plane yesterday. When the plane bumped one little bump, then a second one, I'd felt a frisson of something that I might have called fear if I didn't know better.

I like to fly, and I knew Al couldn't be bothered—a mere plane crash would mean nothing to him. Al would survive anything on this journey that could kill me and my fellow safari passengers.

We were promised lions, rhinos, giraffes, a distant look at all these animals of Mother Earth that were slowly diminishing in number. Al was pleased we were on the way to seeing them in person. So to speak.

My human seatmate was apprehensive. Younger than me by a couple of decades, he was a well-rounded fellow, filling the plane's seat from edge to edge. He didn't quite overflow onto my domain but that was because the armrests were down. He was nervy, the recent bumps eliciting a little yelp.

I said, 'I think of them as corrugations in the air. Just like a ride on a dusty unmade road. Some hard bits for the tyres to get over.'

He gave me a tense grin but didn't reply. I felt Al's response and was pleased I'd made him chuckle.

'I'm a librarian,' I said. 'What's your occupation—' I leaned around to look at his name badge—'Mark?'

'Uh,' he patted his chest as though to settle his heart. The flight was smooth again and he relaxed. 'I'm retired but used to be a chef.' He patted a bit lower down, the belly that projected well in front of him. 'I still cook, and eat.'

He sighed. 'I'm supposed to use this trip to lose a bit. My wife and daughter are over there,' he nodded up the aisle where I could see the tops of two blonde heads, 'this trip is a reward for her, and my daughter and I are along for the ride.'

'Oh? A reward?'

I felt Al stir as Mark talked on. 'Yes, she's a fundraiser for a big charity and recently she did such a great job that a wealthy donor rewarded her with this trip.' He looked at my badge. 'Ah, Randall. Are you still a librarian?'

[He thinks you're much too old to be a librarian.]

I know, I know, I thought back at Al.

'I was a librarian, that's true, but I still am, in a way, still showing and educating.' I paused. 'I have a Passenger with me. Capital P, Passenger.'

Mark turned in his seat as much as he could, which wasn't much, to face me. I'm sure his neck was hurting. His cheeks were flushed. 'Really?'

'Oh yes. For forty years now.'

He was gaping at me—those back teeth on the bottom could use some work—then his mouth shut, and he repeated, 'Really?'

'I bet you thought it was all made up. Are you a denialist? I've been retired for many years, but I assure you my bank account proves Passengers exist.'

'Well, no, I just, I don't know, I've never, you know, met anyone who had one.'

'I can prove it if you like.'

Mark's belly retracted, and his shoulders pulled back. 'Uh, not necessary, thanks.'

I didn't blame him. My Passenger, Al, short for Alien—my little joke—could briefly touch Mark's mind but while it would prove Al's existence to Mark, the resulting freakout just wouldn't be worth it. Mark would need an ambulance and they're in short supply 38,000 feet up.

There were only six of us on safari. I'd paid more than a little extra to have the most luxurious camping available. My ancient bones needed pampering now and then, and a warm bath along with my range of meds kept the arthritis at bay. I was too old to rough it these days. I was comfortable, nearly asleep, when Al said,

[I enjoyed your little joke about corrugations in the air.]

'Mm.' I remembered my pleasure at his reaction. I guess he had double the pleasure, feeling mine. We'd talked about this over the years. In the distance a howl floated into the night air.

[That's a hyena.]

'Mm.'

[Randall.] His tone was forceful. If he were speaking, he'd be loud.

'Mm?'

[It will be tomorrow.]

My eyes opened. The smell of recent rain on the patchy grass and the dusty ground outside filled the cabin and I could see a square of star-filled sky through the window above my bed.

'Tomorrow?'

[There's an old lion not far away. It's attracted to the smells here, animal and human. It can't hunt any more, needs an easy catch, like you.]

'You're not planning on having me eaten by a lion, are you?' I realised I'd said this aloud. I thought, 'Are you?'

[Not exactly.]

When the aliens arrived on Earth, whenever that was—they were undetected for ages—they were desperate to communicate. After many mishaps and some most unfortunate incidents of people being committed to mental institutions, what was happening was gradually understood. Less than three in a billion can link with them and mentally talk with them. I was one of the lucky ones, and my Passenger and I have been together for a long time.

I couldn't have much longer to live; at 87 I'm getting trembly and frail.

On the plane yesterday Mark said, 'Is it, he, with you now? Are you talking to him?'

'Yes. I only speak aloud to him when we're alone. I save the telepathic conversation for times like now when other people are around.'

'Telepathy, huh?'

I nodded.

'Is he always with you?'

'A lot of the time, in recent years. We're like an old married couple, very used to each other.'

'I bet you've done some interesting things.'

My Passenger rides inside my head, seeing, feeling, sensing, everything I do and see and feel. He asks me to experience something for him, like eat a spicy curry. Or spend time among the fish. Luckily for me, he's never been interested in anything voyeuristic. None of them did. Probably something to do with them having no bodies. They love tastes and colours and shapes, they envy the way we humans experience them. Mostly I forget he's there if I'm doing something interesting.

My initial dealings with the alien were handled by our government and I've never known what's in it for them, probably alien science and mathematics. I get truckloads of money for my time and an incredible life.

Al's tastes are wide-ranging. Films, music, a bath, a waterfall. He enjoys autumn leaves and beach balls and fast cars. I have special permission from kindergartens to sit in a corner and watch kids finger-painting. I've spent many an afternoon strolling through art galleries. He loves the Impressionists.

I had, or used to have, an academic sedentary life. A quiet calm person who didn't go adventuring, loved my books and my access to the wide world through computers. I enjoyed helping older people become computer literate, opening that whole world to them. Then Al came along, and I was abseiling (did he want my fear or the abseiling itself, he'd never say), driving Australia's longest straight road where the stars at night spill to the earth, living aboard a submarine, working in the Antarctic—quite a contrast to art galleries and kindergartens.

We've done so much together, for so long, it's become a blur. 'We've done amazing things,' I told Mark, 'things I never thought a librarian would ever do.'

Of course he told his wife and daughter and the other guests, and they were all agog as we settled into the big Land Rover for the visit to the big game reserve. We did see lions, and towering giraffes, and a mother cheetah hunting prey with little ones sneaking along behind her. From our vehicle we spotted hyenas lurking in the long grass.

In a quiet moment George, the former footballer-run-to-seed, asked if my Passenger experienced "highs"—like from drugs, or alcohol, or even the natural high of defeating an opponent. Al suggested I say surviving a dangerous physical challenge is exciting enough, though nothing compares to a drink of water when you're extremely thirsty.

'Look, a herd of zebras!' It was the most vocal Mark's young daughter had been. Everyone else was gazing at me, in awe of what I had within me, missing out on the sight. Al had me watching the zebras intently and we both knew that the zebra group was called a zeal, or a dazzle, not a herd. I was about to show off my knowledge, but Mark's wife (had I heard her name? the fundraiser) asked if Al would appear to them.

He did so briefly, flickering in and out of sight in front of them for a few moments.

The discussion then centred on how a ball of light could contain a person, his soul, his essence. I could feel Al mentally shrugging.

The sixth member of our troupe, Jules the staid accountant on his first trip abroad, wanted to know about Al's velocity. Could he be on Mars, say, in an instant, or did it take time? The answer to that, I relayed for Al, was that it could be either.

Mark's wife said, 'Do you think your Passenger would talk to a group of people at a fundraising function? Oh, I mean, would you, uh, do you or your Passenger do things like that?' She was happy with the promise of a card for future contact.

When I told them Al couldn't wait to see a tree full of monkeys, they couldn't know he thought the Land Rover was full of chattering human primates.

And now it's nearly over. I lie with my eyes open, sleep a distant prospect. This could be my last night on earth. I feel Al stir but he doesn't say anything. He's promised fair warning and he's promised no pain, or very little. Death by lion is unlikely, then.

That howl sounds again, and a snuffling, like a boar outside a tent in the Australian outback, or a bear rifling through rubbish in the Canadian forest.

I have tonight. Then it's morning and I wake and move with a groan. My joints ache. I grimace. I have indigestion and try to burp.

[Decision to make. Randall.]

'I hear you. Remind me again of my choices.' As if I didn't know. As if I hadn't decided already.

[Your body is like the old lion's, Randall. Worn out. Nearing its end. Today, the old lion will startle you and your heart will give up its fight.] He'd never put it quite so starkly. [You may die a normal human death and I will be sad. Or you may go with me. You will be young in that life and may survive for thousands of years.]

Once, he'd asked me to experience a sunrise for him. [We travel the universe. We visit planets and dive into suns and the energies of the galaxies enrich us, but we cannot experience them as you do. I have heard that sunrise on Earth is the most beautiful thing.]

Together we'd enjoyed many a sunrise and now I'd seen my last. But I will go with him, bodiless, a glowing ball of energy but still myself, to the ends of the galaxies. He'd said we'd travel together as long as I wanted, then I could fly solo.

I guess it's not indigestion I'm feeling. I step outside the cabin into the glorious African morning.

2027 words

THE SOONER THE BETTER

'I'm gonna get a dog.'

Devlin stood facing his mother, hands on his hips. His eyes were red and his nose was running.

'I'm going right now,' he said and began to turn away.

'At least blow your nose before you go,' Bianca said, walking two steps after him and holding out Sel's big handkerchief.

But Dev just wiped his sleeve across his nose and trudged away from her. It took him only twenty steps to reach the chook-wire gate and he climbed up it, his small feet finding ready toe-holds. He reached the top and slung one chubby leg over. Balancing, he looked back at her.

She took it as invitation and caught up to him. His curly blond hair shone in the late afternoon sun and his unsmiling face melted her heart. She tucked the handkerchief into the top of his little collared shirt and he sniffed a deep sniff.

'You know Daddy says there's none around, Devvy. It's so sad that Maxie died, but he was very old and very tired. He hardly ever got up and he stopped eating.'

'Well.' Dev's bottom lip quivered. 'We need a dog, Mummy. A new dog will keep the possums off the roof, and, and, keep the dingoes away.'

'It's a really good idea,' his mother said. 'The trouble is, I haven't heard about puppies getting born anywhere round here. Tell you what,' she said, and Dev leaned against her, beginning to come round, ready to be lifted down because his bottom was getting sore on the top of the gate, 'let's get Dad to ask Ferko about a new dog the next time he comes by.'

The boy allowed her to lift him to the ground. She placed a hand on his shoulder and he didn't shrug it off. They walked together back to the house.

'If I write a note for Daddy to leave on the top paddock gate for Ferko, would you draw a dog on it, and maybe colour it in? That way Ferko won't forget to keep an eye out for a new pup for us.'

Before they reached the door, Dev was holding her hand and smiling up at her and Bianca smiled back.

#

'It's just not fair, Dad. I never go anywhere.'

Moving along the grape vine which was shining greenly in the sun, Devlin was picking out the tiny unwanted sprouts. His father was doing the same to the next row of vines. They were back to back, moving sideways, talking over their shoulders.

'Well, nor do I. Nor does your mum.'

'Yeah, but you're old, and you've probly seen everything you want to see already so you don't want to go anywhere. But I'm only ten, and I want to.'

Sel nodded. 'I know. The trouble is, we can't take you. You need your schooling with Mum. I need the horses here, and your mum and me both have to stay here working. We gotta put food on the table, and with only the chooks for eggs and meat sometimes, we've just gotta keep at the veggie garden and I've gotta get out there and track down possums and pigs for meat. You know all that—and where would we go anyway? We don't know anyone anywhere anymore. '

'That sounds as if it could be poetry.' They turned as Bianca spoke.

Sel grinned at his wife. 'Man of literature, that's me. Time for a break?'

'Yes, I've got lunch ready. Come on in.'

Sel and Devlin turned to follow Bianca up to the house.

'The thing is you're safe here. How d'you think we'd feel if we took you somewhere for a visit, or a holiday, and somebody stole you from us?'

The boy's eyes widened. 'Why would someone want to steal me?'

His parents glanced at each other. His mother said, unsettled, 'Well, there's not a lot of children around, you know. We were very lucky to have you. We didn't think we could have any babies but you came along.' She ruffled his hair, and he twisted under her hand. She returned to the kitchen and Dev and his father could hear her rattling pots and cutlery.

'Why didn't you have any more? I woulda liked a brother, or even a sister.'

'Well, like most people these days, and like most animals except the ones that belong here, well, see, something's stopping babies from being born. That's why we could never got a new dog after Maxie died. There aren't any. Only roos and emus and koalas and wild pigs, they're all having babies okay. But not people. There weren't any more children for us.'

'Chooks have babies.'

'Well,' Sel said with a helpless shrug, 'that's just chooks for you.'

Bianca called, 'Devvy, would you come and help me? Sel, can you find us a beer each?'

'There's only two left so it'll be the last till Ferko turns up,' he called back.

Domestic sounds filled the house and kookaburras and galahs competed for space on the high gums closest to the house. Devlin thoughtfully carried a dish to the table. He plonked it down quickly, and blew on his fingers.

'We could visit some of the kids from radio school,' he said. 'There's fifteen of us all up.'

'But you're scattered all over the state,' Sel said. 'It would take days, if not weeks, to reach the closest, and what would happen to the garden and the chooks? The dingoes'd probably get under the house yard fence and where'd we be then?'

'Have to join one of those communities,' Biance muttered, sitting at the table.

'Huh.' Sel silently shared the second-last beer between them.

'Might have to, one day. '

Devlin looked from one to the other.

#

'I ought to just run away.'

Bianca's heart sank at the pure defiance in her son's eyes. She fully understood the impulse in him. How could she not, when she had left her family to be with Sel when she was only a few years older than Devlin was right now? Sel had been the big attraction, of course, but just getting away from her own family had been a big part of it. To go somewhere she hadn't been before.

But it was so precarious out there now, so lonely, so dangerous.

'Ferko said he'll teach me his trade, he'll show me his route and introduce me to everyone he deals with.' Devlin fought to keep tears from his eyes.

'Devvy, you're only 13. It's just too young to think about living life on the road. Not these days.

'Don't call me Devvy,' he muttered. He picked up another tiny onion and picked at its skin with his thumb nail. He'd never match his mother's speed at skinning them. And he didn't even like pickled onions. He sighed.

Brightening, he thought of another good argument. 'Mum, Ferko's got piles of medical books. He told me he'll teach me everything he can. Did you know he was a medical student when he was young? In his own country?'

'Could we borrow his medical books, do you think?' His mum's face was serious. 'My medical books helped your dad when you were born, and they helped me sometimes, like when you broke your wrist and when I had my troubles. But Ferko's books might cover other things.'

'I think they're in his own language, Russian or Hungarian or something. Why do you want them? Is something wrong?'

'Oh, it's just, well, I'm a bit worried about Dad. He's got these black specks as well as bright flashes going in his eyes all the time.'

'Really? What do they mean?'

'Don't know. That's why medical books might be helpful. Even foreign ones, as long as Ferko's here to read them.'

Bianca leaned over to gather up Devlin's pile of peeled onions. 'You've done well. Thanks. Listen, when you go out to look for eggs, just check the fence closest to the chook shed, would you?'

#

'I'm gonna take off one day. You know that.'

'Devlin Doyle,' his mother said, 'don't even think it. You can't leave your dad and me on our own.'

The teenager looked her in the eye. 'What happens to me when you're both gone? Who'll be on their own then? Really on their own?'

'G'wan,' she said, looking away, looking down at her hands beating the cream, going harder and faster. 'We'll be here for ages yet.'

'One day you won't be. Or Dad.' Dev turned on his heel.

'Don't go far,' she said. 'It'll be dark soon.'

He raised a hand in acknowledgement and strode out the door. He'd be going to the gate to wait for his father, she knew. Hoping for his father. Sel had been gone too long. If he didn't come back, Dev wouldn't be the only one taking off. She couldn't keep this place going on her own—just as Dev couldn't. No one could, on their own.

She snatched up an oven cloth and opened the hot heavy door. The biscuits smelled done but she couldn't see them through the blur in her vision.

If Sel didn't bring flour, if Sel didn't come... If only Ferko hadn't stopped coming. He must have died—and now no one came calling with news of people elsewhere and all kinds of goods and produce to trade. If she didn't have flour, and if Carmel the Cow stopped giving milk... it was too hard to think about. Maybe they should have let Devlin go with Ferko, to bring to isolated people like Sel and herself all those little things that make life a bit easier.

She wondered if it was true that there was a settlement by the Brisbane river just a few k away from the old city. Where people on their own could go, people, women, widowed as she could well be if Sel didn't return.

Dev's excited voice penetrated her thoughts and her heart skipped. Sel was back. They'd have to talk about the future. Maybe Sel'd found some new people, heard about a place where there was a girl who might like Devvy, a place they could all go to. She'd hate to think Dev'd never find anyone, and it would be best to stick together.

After Devlin went to bed, Sel and Bianca sat out on the front porch, trying out their son's latest experiments with home brew. There was enough of a breeze to stir the topmost leaves of the tallest gums, and the stars displayed their tiny lights across the blackness overhead.

Sel said, 'Bushfire somewhere out west. I could smell it on the way back.'

He took a deep sniff. 'Can't smell it now.'

'Just as well.' Bianca topped up their glasses.

Sel said, 'Thank God Ferko brought Dev the makings before he disappeared. This's pretty vile, but it'll get better. '

Bianca took a sip and nodded. She set her glass down. 'Maybe by the time Dev's old enough to appreciate his brews for himself, we'd best be living in a settlement, Sel.'

'I know. Ferko used to sing the praises of that place by the river, close to the city. He reckoned there was quite a crowd there.'

'We'd have plenty to offer, if we took all the chooks, and the books Ferko left me.'

'And the home brew.' Sel sat silently for moment, looking up at the graceful gums against the stars. 'The cow couldn't make it, walking. I'll have to build a cart. High sides. Good for Dev to learn how.' He turned to face her. 'I've been vomiting again, Bee.'

Bianca leaned over to place her hand on his. 'You've lost a lot of weight too. I think we'd better get off to a settlement. They're more likely to have some medical help available. Let's think about timing.'

#

'I can't believe we're finally going.'

Dev couldn't stop moving. He walked around the new cart one more time, rapping its sides with his knuckles, standing on his toes to look over. He was proudest of the wheels he'd found hiding at the back of the far shed. 'Think we'll find a place, Dad?'

He gave Gypsy a firm pat on the back that turned into a caress. He was old, their last horse. Dad thought he'd last the trip. Maybe if there were kids at the settlement, Gypsy could give them rides.

'Yeah.' Sel stood for a moment and shut his eyes. 'We'll find a place.'

'You okay, Dad?' Dev's voice rose and Sel opened one eye.

'At least I can see out of one eye, son. I like to stop now and then to check the other one.' He bent to continue sorting out his tools. He'd be taking them all with him but they needed to be compactly packed. He didn't want the goat stepping on them in the cart. An animal with an injured leg, even one giving milk, might be more handicap than help to a new community.

'Probly just as well Carmel the Cow's not with us any more. She'd be hard to transport. Did you pack the cutlery and your mum's best cups and saucers?' If Dev met a girl who liked him—

When there was no reply, he straightened. Dev was at the house fence, looking across at the tall gum by the creek. The white cross the young man had nailed together was bright in the sunshine. Sel squinted his one good eye to bring it into better focus. He walked over to his son.

'It's a good place for your mum, Dev.'

Dev's eyes were awash. 'She thought you were going to die, Dad. You got so thin with all that vomiting and fever and when you went blind in one eye— ' Nodding to himself, Dev said, 'She was great, wasn't she? She made us promise to go, and now we're going. Like she said, the sooner the better.'

'If we'd gone sooner, she might have got better,' Sel said in a husky voice.

They turned together to look again at the cross set low on the scrubby grass. Dev put his arm around his dad's shoulder. 'Come on, Dad.'

2374 words

ADARA'S SECRET

Mum jumps when I nudge her. She's drying her eyes, sitting in a kind of old-lady pose, shoulders hunched forward in a way that's not like her. She's not taking any notice at all of the passing landscape.

'You shouldn't cry for Adara, Mum. She's made her bed, now she's reaping the wind.'

Mum smiles weakly. 'She's got egg on her face from trying to keep the cake she's eaten.'

We've had a good drive so far and had not a bad lunch at a café in the last small town we came to. They tend to blur together after a while. We've avoided serious topics, but Mum has just mentioned Adara and got tearful at once.

We pass through a town that actually has traffic lights. We have to stop at a red light on the main road for two long trucks filled with restless animals. As they turn in front of us, the stench of the enclosed animals fills our car but Mum doesn't seem to notice. A man in a business suit is sitting on a bench seat near a little park with one arm around a young woman in a bright blue dress, the other stretched along the top of the seat. Her head is on his shoulder, long dark hair flowing across his front. A toddler and his dad are holding hands as they walk along licking ice creams. Loving relationships everywhere I look.

I really know I'm in the bush when the super-wide streets appear. On a corner block, a dusty yard with a high wire fence is filled with brilliantly coloured play equipment and children swarm all over it. A woman moves among the children and I imagine the crispness of her steps on the barely-alive grass. It's a clear bright day. Dry verges on the roadsides and yellowing or brown grass in front yards and paddocks show it's been a long time since rain fell.

Mum is gazing out the window. She's aged in the past few weeks and it shows in her hair. It's still only a little grey but until recently it's been well cared for, shiny. Lately it's got lank, and it looks as though she's stopped using her favourite moisturiser. I sniff the air and can't smell its light perfume. I glance at her hands and they look like an old lady's hands.

I don't understand why she's been crying. When Adara was 17, eight years ago, she had a bastard of a row with Mum, the big final one in a series that started when she was about 13. Then she just vanished. Of course there was an investigation, but the police basically thought she'd run away from home.

'The case won't be closed until she's found,' had been the final reassurance. We hadn't heard from them in years.

I'd always been the more placid of us two children, probably not as vivacious or maybe as interesting a person, but Mum seemed happy having me around. I have my own place a few blocks away from Mum but we eat together a couple of times a week, sometimes see a movie. Women haven't been a big part of my life: I like my own company and don't want a family—not yet anyway. I don't think Mum has had any relationships since Dad left, when Adara was two and I was seven, but I may be wrong.

Mum used to talk about her biological clock, the one that required a grandchild or two. She'd say, 'A woman of my age ought to have a grandchild to run after,' and in principle I agreed. I'd heard somewhere that the world's population was going to go into reverse some time in the late 21st century, and we should all start reproducing like rabbits. I didn't see me doing it and I would wonder occasionally if somewhere out there Mum did have grandchildren, if Adara had a family. Mum and I rarely talked about her—until a fortnight ago when she became our only topic of conversation.

I think Mum is quite possibly the victim of a crazy scam. Crazy because no one's asked her for money yet, but a scam all the same because of what she's been told. She's so gullible. Either that or Adara herself is plotting some fiddle.

Mum says the official who's been to see her wants nothing in writing, nothing recorded, that's why the personal visits only. Now, to me, that's as dodgy as can be. What government agency doesn't want every I dotted and every T crossed? In triplicate?

The story is that Adara was found about six weeks ago by a couple of station hands on horseback in a back paddock of a station out beyond Longreach. She was heavily pregnant and the station hands were weirded out because they couldn't tell how she got there. She claims aliens have had her for eight years.

I thought *a baby will really cramp her style*. But it's a mean thought because how would I know what her style is? She was 17 when I last saw her and now she's 25.

Anyway, the nearest medical facility was a government one, apparently a very secret joint venture between our Department of Defence, ASIO and the CIA. According to Ben Cross, my fellow stock and station agent and an avid UFO fan, Adara sounds like the classic pregnant-by-aliens returned abductee. Hmm.

Ben also claims the facility is a hotbed of secret genetic engineering in Australia and we shouldn't be surprised by whatever offspring Adara produces. Ben really can't lose—it's either alien abduction or government conspiracy, with the CIA thrown in for good measure.

So here we are, Mum and me, both of us taking time off work, on our way across country in my little runabout to the secret joint venture facility.

'Marcus,' Mum says. I glance at her. 'There's something I have to tell you about Adara. A couple of things, actually, that might change your attitude.'

'Oh yes?'

It would have to be something pretty spectacular to make me eager to be here, something that would convince me that Mum wasn't nuts, that it wasn't just a huge con cooked up maybe by Adara herself with a few friends. A sudden arrival at the back of beyond! I can just picture it—a barren stretch of land at the back of beyond festooned with roo scat, dingo droppings, and scrub.

'That government man who told me about Adara has been to see me more often than I've told you. I didn't tell you before because I needed to think things through myself first.'

The westerly sun is shining right in my eyes so I lower the visor. The road ahead is like a thick line of black ink with jagged brackets of dead wallabies punctuating it here and there. Maybe they're small kangaroos.

I know Mum is looking at me

'There's something else …' She's struggling to speak, swallowing drily.

'Here.' I thrust the bottle of water at her. 'C'mon, have a drink and spit it out.'

Mum reaches for the bottle and slowly takes off the lid. She drinks deeply, has a second swallow. She screws the top back on and places the bottle in the door at her side, saying quietly, 'Spit in one hand and wish in the other, and see which one you have the most in.'

'Good one, Mum,' I say just as quietly.

'Ok, no more mucking about. Marcus, Adara's dying.'

Mum gulps a swallow of air and her face crumples. Her handkerchief comes up to cover her entire face and she turns away to the window again.

My mouth falls open. My mind is buzzing, refusing to take in what she's said. All I can think is *Adara's upsetting us yet again*. I'm sitting beside my grieving mother and I'm thinking, *damn you, Adara, this is the biggest thing yet.*

Mum's looking at me again and I shake my head, sharply, quickly.

'Mum,' I say. Unexpectedly, stunningly abruptly, Mum's face blurs and I realise my eyes are filling.

I manoeuvre the car off the road and stop, stupefied. Where have these tears come from? I haven't thought about Adara since I don't know when, haven't wanted to, thought us both well off without her and her selfish ways. Now, I'm crying.

I can't see the roadside, only the picture in my mind. The picture fills my arms and I'm sitting in a squashy lounge chair, the old green floral-print cushions enfolding me, and enclosed, cuddled, hugged in my arms is little baby Adara. I can smell the clear baby skin, the powder, the milky sweetness on her breath. Mum has just finished feeding her and it's my job, the big brother's job, to mind the new little sister who can't do anything by herself, not one single thing, *not even lift her own head up*, Mum says, *you have to hold her head and be her support*, Mum says.

One day, Mum says, no it's Dad, he's leaning over the back of the lounge, I can smell his special smell, his shaving cream and aftershave smell, one day, he says, *this little sister will be your best friend in the whole world. You'll play together, you'll have secrets together, you can teach her things, you'll be the best friend of each other all your lives and you'll protect her.*

In the here and now, Mum's hand touches my cheek and I lean into her palm. She reaches up then to put an arm around my shoulder and we rest our heads together. I find my own handkerchief, dab at my eyes. Take a deep inflating breath.

'Mum, you said, *a couple of things*?'

'Right.' She turns to face me. 'You know Adara's going to have a baby, but, but she can't survive the birth.' She holds up a hand. 'No, they don't say why. But she wants us to have the child once she's gone, but specially you. Adara says she wants you to, to adopt—'

Mum gulps again and scrubs at her eyes with her scrunched up handkerchief. I lean over and open the glovebox in front of her, fetch out a narrow box of tissues.

Me, a parent? My own tears dry as I quickly think about this. Practical thoughts shoot through my mind—work, house, baby clothes, vaccinations, pink frills. I can see myself holding a baby again. This time we will stay friends, and I won't let anything come between us. We will love and respect each other.

But not Adara, another baby.

'Mum, has she got a name yet?'

Mum's sigh is relieved but her face looks wary, uneasy. 'No, they're not sure of the baby's sex.'

'Of course! It could be a boy!' How dumb can I get? I see myself at soccer practice, yelling support, camping, surfboards. I know I'm avoiding emotion by thinking of practicalities. But vaccinations are essential after all.

I start the car and we drive on. This is an amazingly good road for such an isolated place. The surface is so smooth, perfectly canted. Occasional prickly pears are the tallest thing in sight. There's no wind, no movement anywhere except our car.

Abruptly I realise that I have fully accepted that wherever she's been all this time, Adara's back. It sounds as though she hasn't long to live but we'll see her and talk to her. If there's time we'll reconcile, she and Mum will reconcile, we'll be adults coming together in a way we never did, never could, before.

But she's going to die. We'll work to get over it, then I'll have her son to raise. I'll be a babe in the woods, wet behind the ears, raising a son. Raising a son to enjoy clichés with me, and with his grandma.

'One more thing.' Mum sounds deadly serious now. 'There's something you have to think about hard before we arrive. In fact, I think we might stay overnight at a motel and arrive at the place, the centre, tomorrow morning.'

I find myself frowning. What else could need to be thought about *hard*? Adara's turned up, she's pregnant, she's dying, I get to bring up her son, her daughter, if I choose to. More than enough to think about, *hard*.

Mum takes a deep breath. 'If you keep the baby, you'll have to stay there for a while.'

I stare at her, holding the wheel steady on the straight road.

'For the foreseeable future. Possibly years.'

I realise I'm still staring at her so I wrench my gaze back to the road.

'That government official was very uncomfortable about telling me and I don't know the full story, but they want Adara's baby to be kept a secret.'

'What? No way! If I adopt Adara's baby, he should come and live with me so we can be a family. What reason did he give, this official?'

'He didn't give any, really. I talked to him about the alien aspect of it, about Adara's claim to have been abducted, but he just laughed. He scoffed, really. It was embarrassing. I think he was trying to hint that the reason they would want to keep the baby secret was because of genetic engineering. But he didn't sound very convincing.'

'Why tell you anything at all, then?'

'I don't know.' Mum sounds both exasperated and annoyed. 'Maybe we'll find out when we get there. I hope we will. There must be some reason they want you and me involved.' Mum's voice sounds a bit panicky with this last statement and it makes me nervous.

The road ahead rises with the suddenly undulating landscape, a change at last from the flat surfaces we've been seeing. There's a town, a village, some distance ahead. There won't be a rest area for a while, so I pull over off the road, gravel crunching and spinning out from under my wheels.

Mum's fingers are destroying tissues fresh out of the packet. First one, then another, and another.

'You've got more to tell me, haven't you?'

Throwing the tissues down on the floor by her feet, she nods, saying, 'Let's stretch our legs.'

She's out of the car before I can undo my seatbelt. When I'm out and turn to look at her, she's leaning against the car, hands flat on the top above her door. I didn't know knuckles could turn white in that position.

'Marky.' Adara's baby nickname for me keeps me quiet. Mum doesn't often use it. 'When that official talked to me that last time, he came back after I'd shut the door. He came back and he said, *Mrs Campion, don't be afraid.*'

'Afraid of what?'

Mum doesn't hear me. She's saying to herself, 'No, that's not right. The word was *frightened.*' Her face darkens with an emotion I can't name. 'His actual words were, *please don't be frightened.*'

2496 words

THE YEAR I TURNED 12

2044. That was the year I nearly met another child for the first time, and nearly got a sister or a brother, and nearly lost my dad. The possibility of the other child was the most interesting thing to me at the time.

When I came upon the diary I started when I was nine, it started me thinking about the year I turned 12. 2044.

There had been plans for me to meet the two girls and the six boys in my computer classes, but that was before I went down with glandular fever, and before the big cyclone killed the electricity for weeks.

Until I learned about populations and low birth rates and low fertility, I used to harass Mum and Dad about a baby brother or sister. I speculated in the diary about what a fantastic variety there must have been among the millions of children in the Australia that used to be. I knew kids from movies and books and my interactive online lessons, but I'd never met one.

It's strange to think that if I'd lived back in old Brisbane, I might have been a featherbrained pink-and-pretty princess, pestering my parents for the latest teenage fashions. Or I might have been sporty, swimming in summer and in winter maybe played rugby, the sport Mum played. I might have camped out, climbed trees, not bothered by scraped knees and mozzies in the dark. Who can tell?

Or I might have been the greedy reader I still am today. I read then, and read now, because my dream—to travel, see the world—wasn't, and isn't, possible. As impossible as meeting other children when I was still a child myself.

So, the year I turned 12 was the year I nearly met another child for the first time, and nearly got a sibling, and nearly lost my dad. It would take another three years before I met another child, and by then I wasn't a child any more myself.

The diary noted how tired and weak I was after my long illness. One night I turned over in bed and blinked with sore eyes at a candle's wavery light in the doorway. From the shape and height, I knew who it was though I couldn't see the green eyes and the grey-streaked auburn hair that Dad called rusty.

'Bernie.' My voice was croaky.

Briefly, the weather was both audible and visible. Lightning flashed behind her and I could hear rain on the roof and against the windows. Funny how it had just vanished from my hearing. I asked myself in the diary how I could forget a cyclone that had already lasted more than two months—if I hadn't lost track of time and it was even longer.

I don't remember asking anyone how a cyclone could last months—'super cyclone' seemed to cover it well. Since then, of course—well, nowadays weather imprisons more people than tyrants ever did.

My great-aunt Bernie carefully placed the candle on its saucer on the bedside table and sat on the edge of the bed. When she leaned over to kiss my forehead, I reached up sleepily for a hug. I still remember my shock when my stiff fingers caught in the scarf behind her head and it slid off backwards. Bernie's head was naked. Totally bald and paler than her face. The skin was so smooth, a contrast to the wrinkles around her eyes.

Bernie was the oldest person I knew. I was the youngest.

'What happened?'

She pulled the scarf forward over her head and undid the large loose knot that my fingers had found. 'This is part of my current disguise.'

I was so tired. 'I can't stay awake. Will I see you tomorrow?'

'No. I've got a job to do. Don't know how long I'll be. Your dad will be with me, so don't worry.'

She leaned over to kiss my forehead again, and then she was gone.

Her visit had woken me up a bit mentally. I lay in bed, beginning to be a bit hungry, losing the sound of the rain again, dozing, and thought about my great-aunt Bernie and her tricks. A bald head of all things. Usually, Bernie dyed her greying auburn hair a bright orange 'so people can see me coming.' But Dad told me one day that there was another reason for Bernie to be so obvious and eye-catching.

'When she puts on a grey wig and hunches over like an old lady, no one knows it's her. She's our secret weapon.'

No one sat me down and told me what Bernie and Dad actually did, but I'd figured out most of it. It was so dangerous, so risky. What if one of them got hurt? I used to worry, but Mum always said they were big enough to look after themselves. I should concentrate on what concerned me. As if Dad and Bernie didn't concern me!

I know from my diary what I dreamed that night. Later, I figured it was prompted by knowing that Bernie and Dad had been in danger other times when they'd had 'a job to do'.

In the dream, I was watching from a high place, seeing myself holding the brown hands of a boy on one side and a girl on the other. It's funny to think that in the years since then I would have forgotten the dream completely, as so many others have been forgotten. But I wrote it down.

We all had bald heads and our feet were bare. We were dancing, or stomping, on grass, bells somewhere in the background providing music and rhythm.

My diary notes 'my belly felt sick' when the boy and girl were pushed away by shadowy soldiers in uniforms holding long guns. I tried to call out but my throat was too dry. The bells faded to a gentler sound.

When I opened my sticky eyes I could still hear bells. I was confused until I realised they were the bells of the church two blocks away. I hadn't been dancing at all, hadn't been with a boy and girl as brown as the men and women that Dad and Bernie help to bring to Brisbane.

I noticed the wind—the rain must have eased a bit—the house seeming to shift a little with the gusts against the walls. Mostly the high fence protected the house from winds, but these were Cyclone Winds. That's how I wrote about them, with capitals.

When I woke properly it was daytime but the light was muted by the falling rain. I realised I had more energy, that the headache was not so strong, and my throat didn't hurt as I drank. The sound of my teeth clattering against my glass reminded me of the bells, and my dream. I lay there and daydreamed about having friends like those brown children. I might have mixed up the dream with the daydream. I know I would've wished very hard just to see another child right in front of me, someone I could hear and smell and know.

I lay there mentally writing in my diary about Bernie's visit in the night. And her bald head. I tried to disregard any danger Bernie and Dad might be in.

Much of it I did write later, about my dream, and Bernie's night visit before she went away with Dad.

The next time I woke there was another sound in the distance, penetrating through wind and rain. It was the chant from the mosque down the block, a sound I used to hear every day, unlike the church bells which rang only on a Sunday. I could hear the prayer-caller's patter playing through its cycle, calling the faithful to prayer. The morning seemed well along, so it might be the second of the five times it would play during the day.

There were other sounds that I hadn't heard since the bad weather began. I tried to remember how long it had been since strident white cockatoos had attacked the African tulip seed pods—our orange-flowered tree was probably torn apart—and I wondered how the galahs were faring that used to make a raucous racket outside my window. They'd probably all fled inland to the safety of drier weather.

I thought about the baby kookaburra that had spent four hours one Sunday morning on a branch near my window, changing position every few minutes as it practised getting its balance right.

I must have been really bored as the diary was quite detailed sometimes.

The door clicked open and Mum peeked around the edge of it. 'You're awake,' she told me. (My diary says, 'Sometimes mothers say the most obvious things.')

'I've looked in half a dozen times and you've been asleep. How do you feel?'

'Much better. But still headachy.' I struggled to sit up. 'I'm sick of it.'

Right out of the blue, I started to feel irritable. I'd been happy to doze, but now I felt like complaining. 'When is that going to stop?' I meant the sounds of the caller-to-prayer.

Mum sat on the edge of the bed. 'I'm glad to hear it. It means the weather's calming down, maybe the cyclone is starting to fade away.'

She raised her eyebrows. 'Aren't you surprised to hear it? I mean, we haven't heard it for some time.'

I just looked at her.

'There's no electricity so how come we can hear the call?'

I was suspicious. 'You know the answer, don't you?'

Mum grinned. 'Just trying to get your brain working. Dad says they've got hold of the man with the most powerful voice to call the people to prayer. He was talking to that carpenter he knows, what's his name, Ahmed?'

I listened a bit longer, and had to agree. I'd just assumed it was the normal loudspeaker. I lay back on my pillow.

'When am I gonna get better? I've been lying here for days.'

'You can get up whenever you like. Do you want to try?'

'Yes.'

I knew I wouldn't make it as far as the door, but I'd said I wanted to, so I had to try. I was shocked by the jelly-like quiver in my legs.

After that I was happy to vegetate, my quiet room an oasis of tranquillity compared with what was happening outside. My eyes were closed and I didn't move when the bedroom door opened.

'She's asleep, Danny. The news will keep.'

I started to roll back over but the door shut with a quiet whoosh-click, cutting off Mum's voice. When I woke yet again I had more energy and was even able to sit up. Mum kept me company, folding laundry that she had washed the old-fashioned way, by hand, and had dried on racks and the backs of chairs all through the house. She told me all about it. Mum said we were very lucky we had a gas stove, to have hot food.

'Mum, what news were you talking to Dad about?'

I was sitting up at last, with a tray on my lap. Mum was tempting my appetite with my favourite, little curried egg sandwiches.

'Did you hear us? I thought you were asleep.' She flapped a sheet open, swishing it through the air then rapidly halved and halved it again, and slapped it down on top of a pile of others and came to sit on the bed.

I remember these details so clearly. I think I do. Images spurred by phrases in my diary.

'Dad and Bernie have gone back to the islands. They and their group are going by boat to the Indonesian coast and they've got a good plan, apparently. They'll be launching well north so the cyclone won't affect them.'

'Maybe not, but what about soldiers over there?' I remembered my dream.

'Your dad isn't worried, so I'm not either. We all hope they have a successful trip and get back safely. To make you feel better about it, I'll give you some news, something really good.'

Mum patted my leg through the cover. 'You know usually it's grownups who try so hard to reach Australia, trying desperately to get away from the awful conditions?'

I nodded. Not just Indonesia either.

'This time, they expect to bring back a group of children.' I remember Mum laughed. 'You should see your face.'

Light abruptly flickered overhead and vanished. 'Maybe the power's coming back at last.'

'What about the children?' I asked her. Surely that wasn't the end of the story.

'If this trip is successful, they'll bring back a group of orphans, kiddies probably younger than you who have no relations at all. They're in what passes for an orphanage, dreadful conditions Bernie says. Most of them are boys, who are wickedly neglected. But there are a few girls and Bernie says the government wants them in particular. Our government.'

I knew about girls being precious. I ought to know, locked away in the family compound, never seeing anyone but my immediate family, constantly aware that some people try to steal any girls they could find unguarded.

'What will happen to the orphans?' My concern about Dad and Bernie had melted away.

'Bernie says if the children can be rescued, we'll adopt one. Boy or girl.'

Mum was smiling at me. 'There's that stunned face again,' and she leaned across the bed to touch my nose. 'That's Dad's news.'

I felt better over the next few days. I was so exhilarated by the wonderful news that I was inspired to get out of bed. The power had come back on, and I went online to reunite with my classmates the next day. It was always hard keeping the secret about Dad and Bernie's activities but this time it was particularly trying. Then I caught up with my diary entries, the dream and the bells and the prayer-caller and everything, and I started a list of the toys I didn't want any more. I'd love to give them to a new little sister. Or brother.

A few days later the bell on the inside of the kitchen door rang abruptly. Mum went to the intercom on the kitchen wall and spoke briefly, then pressed the button that opened the big outer gate in the compound wall.

'That was Doctor Lingiari.' My heart sank at the look on her face. She came back to the table where I was sitting. 'He's coming in to wait for Dad and Bernie. Your dad's been shot.'

'Is he ok?' I thought my heart would break through my chest.

Mum looked around as though she didn't know what to do next. Her eyes were distant.

'We should get the storeroom ready. He said we should fix up a bed for Danny in there.' She turned to leave, adding, 'He was shot in the thigh, but he's had medical attention. It could be worse.'

Doctor Lingiari arrived in a whirl of activity and sent Mum to gather bandages and to boil water. He took time to ruffle my hair and to look at my face. His eyes were so black in his brown face I couldn't see the pupils. I wrote that in my diary more than once.

'You look pretty good, mate,' was all he said.

Mum's eyes were glittering, with tears or excitement or worry, I couldn't tell. My breath was coming fast and shallow and my head began to hurt. Why did Dad have to be looked after in the storeroom? Not a normal bedroom?

Mum hurried back and was busy collecting stuff from cupboards. She flung words at me. 'Grab what you need from your room. We'll be settling in the storeroom.'

'Why?' I stood up and put my pen and diary into my dressing gown pocket.

Mum threw to me the zippered bag of Band-Aids and bandages and other first aid things. 'Take this into the storeroom. You could sort them by size. Wash your hands on the way.'

I detoured to my bedroom and snatched up my pillow and stuffed some things inside its cover. Books, two teddies, Dad's old iPod in case I was allowed batteries for it. I held the pillow and the first aid bag between my feet while I washed my hands then headed for the storeroom.

I could hear Mum and the doctor talking quietly together by the bed that was waiting for Dad. They were afraid soldiers might have traced him and Bernie.

The storeroom was our safe room, solidly reinforced with locks on the inside. It was kept stocked with food and water. Beds, a portable toilet and lots of books, with candles, gas cylinders, torches and boxes of batteries. We'd lived in there for six full days when the big cyclone started until we found our house was built to take the battering.

Why did we need to hide away in the storeroom now? And where were the children? I turned to Mum and asked.

She looked at Dr Lingiari, who shook his head. 'No children were saved this time,' he said.

As it turned out, we didn't need to stay in the storeroom at all. No soldiers or anyone else came looking for Dad or Bernie—but Dad almost lost his leg and he almost succumbed to a raging fever before Dr Lingiari rounded up extra antibiotics from somewhere. No children were rescued for three years, and by then I was well resigned to not meeting any. No one my age was rescued to become my brother or sister.

Now, of course, my school is filled with little brown orphans who are fascinated by stories from the old days. And here's my diary, just bursting with the tales I wrote down—stories from my mum and dad, and my great-aunt Bernie. She is still the oldest person I know, but I'm no longer the youngest.

2994 words

KAM AND NOX

Kam and Nox turned for a final wave, but the boatman was already preparing to recross the river.

'That was great!' Nox said as he hurried after Kam. 'Can we do it again? We can pay, can't we?'

'Sorry, mate, no time,' Kam said. 'Have to get a move on, reach Mrs H's tomorrow.'

Nox kicked at a chunk of concrete and watched it fly along the ground. He stomped his feet and felt better.

'Why's it called a punt?'

Kam shrugged. 'One of the old names. Mrs H'd know.'

'What's this place called again?'

'Willemjolli I think.'

'Has the river got a name?'

'Brizba, somethin like that.'

'D'you think there's sharks?'

'Dunno.'

Nox hurried to catch up. 'You want me to shut up?'

'Just for a bit till I see if I remember the way.'

The boys pushed their way through the scrub, stepping over broken bits of weedy paved areas and brushing away the sticky black bushflies. With daylight fading, mozzies wouldn't be far away.

The punt across the river had been fun, the old man letting them both have a go at pulling on the thick rope that crossed the river at an angle. The northern end of the punt's crossing started at what used to be the city centre which the boys knew was a place to avoid. There were too many gangs hanging out in the remnants of some buildings. Nox always figured he'd end up with one of them since the only alternative seemed to be working in the gardens and scavenging, like his dad. Nox didn't fancy that at all.

He'd never thought he'd go and live with Mrs H the way Kam had done for a while, and Elly before him. Nox wondered if Mrs H was as ancient as the old man on the river punt.

Nox knew the derelict city spaces were dangerous for another reason. Some of the still-standing walls could fall suddenly, the last of the metal reinforcement inside finally collapsing to powder. With a mental quiver Nox remembered Kam's mum talking about metal powder, how it filled the air so much that people died where they stood, their lungs clogged beyond aid or recovery.

This southern point of the punt's course led to the traces of what Elly called a bikepath, through a bushy area that was empty of people. She said they'd be on the right track if they saw faded images on the path made out of two circles with a triangle between them, and sometimes the outline of a person above the triangle. Kam said he'd learned about triangles and circles and squares, but he'd forgotten until Elly reminded him. Nox didn't know about them at all. None of them had ever seen a bike except in megzines and newspapers.

The other thing the boys watched out for was the old road, the threeway. If they came to it, they'd have to change direction a bit. Nox was glad they didn't have to cross it. Gangs patrolled the road and you had to pay a toll. Elly had given them extra stuff just in case. Elly was smart. And now a baby was growing inside her and Kam would be an uncle when he was only twelve.

Kam swore loudly at a dingo sprinting in front of them, adding, 'Watch out, there might be more.' Nox moved closer. Kam'd look after him.

Kam and Elly and their mum had been Nox's neighbours all his life. He'd miss them while he stayed at Mrs H's place. Nox had whined about having to live with an old lady, no matter how many books and stuff she had, but privately he was looking forward to learning to read better, and to finding out why things in the world were so different from the old days. His dad said he always regretted not learning to read properly and he wanted better for his boy.

'What's it like at Mrs H's?' Nox realised he'd spoken aloud when Kam answered.

'It's real intresting. Heaps of rooms under the ground—'

'G'wan.'

'No, true. They're all dug out and there's plastic pipes that bring water to the house and there's special rooms filled with heaps of food on shelves cause everyone works in the gardens between lessons and it's great.'

'What about the house?'

'Well it's wood a'course but not like your place or mine. The wood's all smooth and nice. It was made, the house I mean, in the old days. By Mrs H's family, I think.'

The boys fell silent again, listening to birds high above and mysterious rustlings in the low scrub they had to push aside to see the bikepath. Nox looked at Kam's backpack, bobbing up and down in front of him. It had something special in it, Kam's mum's special treasure. Elly had promised before their mum died that she'd take it to Mrs H but now Elly was busy with Jimbo and with being pregnant. So Kam was taking both Nox and his mum's special treasure to Mrs H.

'It's getting dark. How're the eggs? We'll probly need em first thing in the mornin.'

Nox said, 'They're okay.'

'Good. What about here? The big tree'll give us a bit of shelter and the bush'll hide us if anyone comes.'

'Yeah, looks okay. We can get up that other tree, the littler one, if dingoes come sniffin.'

'Bloody things,' Kam said impassively, patting the solid nulla nulla that Jimbo had given him. Dingoes had better watch out, Nox thought.

'I'll put the eggs up in this fork. Don't think ants'll get through the paper.'

Beginning to tie their canvas shelter by a stringy extension to a low bush behind the big gum, Kam glanced across at Nox. 'Make sure you close the bag tight. Keep the smell inside.'

'Yeah.'

The boys settled side by side under the canvas roof and chewed on strips of dried beef with hard little apples to follow.

Nox asked Kam, 'Do you think it's true what Elly says? That in the old times you could go into a place and buy food? Or pay other people to cook for you? Or fly in the sky in a plane? Or just get in a car and drive anywhere you liked? Anywhere in the whole country?'

'Don't be stupid, of course it's true. Mum told us. You seen pictures in the old megzines. If you climb to the top of that in daylight,' he nodded up at the big gum, 'you'll see the old threeway road that goes around the whole country. Mum used to say it had thousands of cars on it every day.'

'Gee,' Nox started but Kam went on, 'You seen the picture Elly's got, the one with thousands of people all standin up and wavin their arms about at football. Like when we have a game and people come and watch. But in the old days, there were millions of people around so thousands watching football, that's fair enough, and thousands drivin too.'

Kam wriggled a hip, searching for a comfortable spot in the hard earth. 'Let's get some sleep. You can ask Mrs H all about the old days if you want.' He paused. 'Once we get past the Pickets.'

Nox ignored that. 'I wonder if they used a pig's bladder for a football in the old days.'

Kam didn't reply. There was silence for a moment then Nox said quietly, 'I forgot to put socks over our shoes. Sorry.'

'Don't worry. You can check 'em in the morning. If you get bit, I'll suck the poison out—but not if you get bit on your bum.'

Nox laughed.

Morning arrived with light and sound. The light was gentle, filtering through the high open canopy of the tall gum and the closer-set branches of the lower scrubby trees; the sound was loud and raucous. Nox shifted to one elbow and sat up. Holding the canvas opening aside he looked out. He couldn't see Kam, just Indian mynahs darting about, screaming at two crows sitting calmly together on a high branch. Suddenly a big granddaddy kookaburra dived through branches to the ground, scattering the mynahs, then it rose with a couple of downstrokes, a small green snake curving from its beak. The crows suddenly turned in tandem to look northward and Nox couldn't help swivelling his head a fraction of a second later to look too, and then felt foolish. He was facing the trunk of a sapling gum, black ants flowing up and down its mottled surface.

Alert for more snakes, Nox was crawling out from the canvas when Kam called. 'C'mon lazybones, let's get goin. I've got the eggs, you pack the canvas away. Let's keep an eye out for kai along the way. There's banana trees somewhere soon and we can try those mandarins we got yesterday. You got the jerky handy? And let's open one water bottle for now, save the other for later.'

An hour later, tired, Nox lifted his head. 'Kam, listen.'

'What?'

'Stop a minute. Hear it? Sounds like a waterfall. We could swim.'

'Too cold. No time.'

'Spit!' Nox fancied a swim. 'What if I go and catch up with you later?'

'You'd get lost.'

'I would not! I c'n foller a path as good as you.'

Kam stopped then. He turned and faced Nox, nearly tripping on a wayward vine that mostly paralleled the path but here flowed across it. 'If you got lost, you'd walk and walk, gettin loster and loster. And then what? You're only nine, so after a bit you'd sit down and cry. And then what?'

'Aw, I would not.'

'And then what, mate? What would hear you cryin? And call its mates? And come sneakin along to find you? Goodbye Nox. Happy full-belly dingoes.'

'Awright,' Nox growled. 'Let's keep goin.'

When they came to a moss-coated brick arch opening under an overhead roadway, Kam veered away from it.

'Picket territory now,' he said quietly, adding nervously, 'That open part back there,' and both boys glanced back at it, 'is only standin cause it was built in the convict days. Made by jammin bricks together so tight they can't fall down.'

'What's convict days?'

Glad to be distracted, Kam only said, 'Boy, Mrs H'll have a lot to teach you.'

'G'wan,' Nox scoffed, 'you only know cause Elly told you.'

'Yeah, but Mrs H told her.'

Then two Pickets were in front of them. Two of the first-ones, skinny black men with narrow wooden spears taller than themselves placed firmly on the ground at their sides. Nox stood immobile, his eyes on the sharp points of the stone flints above the men's heads. Kam swallowed and raised a hand in greeting.

'Goin to see Mrs H,' he said. 'We got the toll.' He nodded at the bag on Nox's back.

Staring up at the men with big eyes, Nox blurted, 'We got to see Mrs H. It's really important. We got to give her somethin special. She's spectin us.'

'Izzat so? What sort of somethin special?'

Kam nodded at Nox. 'I'm takin him to stay with Mrs H.'

The impassive faces just looked at him.

'Aw, you know how Mrs H talks about metal, about if anyone finds some she wants to know about it? Well, my Mum found some and when she was dyin she made my sister Elly promise to take it to Mrs H.' Kam took a breath.

The taller of the two asked, 'Is that Elly who's Jimbo's mate? She's childin, eh? Good news.'

'Yeah!' Nox was amazed.

'Jimbo's me cousin. That's not his real name, a'course, but …' scornfully, 'you couldn't even say it.'

Nox saw Kam relax a bit, so he did too. 'When Elly has the baby, we'll be sort of related, eh? I'm Kam, this's Nox.'

The shorter man grunted. He said something in an aside to his mate and pivoting on one heel disappeared into the bush. The other man relaxed his spear against his side and beckoned them to follow him.

'Give us your toll,' he said shortly. 'I'll put you on the right path.'

Nox was going to say Kam knew the way, but thought better of it. He tugged the canvas bag to his front and opened its leather tie, his feet tripping over thin tree roots across the trail. The tall black man's footsteps were inaudible as he trod ahead of them. Nox got out the packet of eggs and looked across at Kam.

'How many?' he mouthed.

Kam frowned. ''Scuse me, mate.'

Their guide stopped. 'Me name's Warroo. What?'

'We got eggs for the toll. Fresh yesterday from the hens. How many d'you want?'

Warroo dropped his head to one side, considering. 'How many you got?'

Nox said, 'We got to keep some for Mrs H,' as Kam replied, 'Twenty four.'

'Don't want Mrs H missin out. Give us ten.' Warroo turned and started his steady pacing again.

#

Nox knew that Mrs H had a special reason for wanting to see metal but Kam wouldn't tell Nox what it was. Kam said it was Mrs H's story to tell, if she wanted to. Nox tried hard not to stare at Mrs H while Kam talked, but he'd never seen anyone so old. She was so little and wrinkly and her skin looked so like thin white paper that Nox felt the urge to touch it. He reckoned it would feel dry and crinkle under his fingertips. By the light of the long candle inside a wood-framed box with glass sides, Mrs H's skin had some of the whiteness of Elly's skin when she exposed usually-hidden bits of it to the sun. Nox was more used to the skin colours of people with some first-people colour in them, like Elly's baby would have. Nox hadn't thought about it before but he was thinking now there's not many just-white-skin people around. There used to be heaps, you could see it in the old megzines that Elly had, and the fallen-down pictures all over the place. Ads, Elly called them.

Some of the megzines had pictures of people who were really fat, too. Nox had never seen a fat person.

The boys had eaten and found their room and they'd met a bewildering number of people, all of them living and working at Mrs H's, some students, some teachers. After dark as Kam made sure Elly's cloth-wrapped package was safe, Nox found himself looking forward to going to bed. It would be his first time sleeping in a real bed, one like in the pictures in the megzines. It was a wooden bed with legs keeping it off the floor, with a mattress, and sheets and proper pillows.

Now, after the others had finished breakfast, Nox was watching the smiling woman from the kitchen take away their dishes. Nox had never been waited on like that. The clear windows revealed tidy gardens in the morning light, with a backdrop of high gums, jacarandas, and a towering African tulip. A goat and a sheep were standing back to back on the grass, as though refusing to look at each other.

As they waited, there were voices outside and in other rooms. The kitchen woman called, 'Mrs H says you can go for a wander inside, have a look around. She'll come and find you.'

As they wandered from room to room, Nox couldn't hide his amazement at all he was seeing. He stroked the edges of a pale brown chest of drawers and asked Kam, 'How come she 'nt bin raided?' He'd never seen such pale wood.

Kam shrugged. 'Well, the first-ones look after her. The Pickets specially. But none of the gangs'd touch her, you know, 'cause they need to see her sometimes.'

'Not the first-ones, I bet, they wouldn't need to see her.'

'Well, no, they got their own things. They just don't need what us white people need. We couldn't live in the bush the way they do.'

Kam looked up at high shelves with dusty boxes visible. 'I guess everyone knows she's got what's needed in a mergency. There's not a lot of us people left, white people…'

'Yeah.'

'… and there's no doctors or other skillers like that, and Mrs H's got heaps of stuff. You name it, she's got it.'

'What, like, like glasses for people with bad eyes? Or like, um, crutches?'

'I dunno about crutches, most people can make a crutch out of a stick. But she's sure got glasses. Boxes and boxes. Every time someone finds some in the dust, they bring'm to her, and she saves them. She saves everything. I got Mum's glasses for her. I remember when I had to tie the sides of the glasses to the front part with bits of fishing line because I could see better than her.

Mum said tiny metal screws used to do the job.' Kam shook his head. 'Those screws must have been really, really tiny.'

'What else's Mrs H got?'

'Look, boxes of wool, all colours, and plastic or wood needles to work it, and heaps of shoes, and packets of seeds for planting. Probly most of them won't take, too old. There's clothes, all sorts, and books, thousands and thousands of books.'

Nox nodded thoughtfully, gazing around him.

'Paper, pencils, wood tools…'

'Yeah, yeah.'

Kam added, 'Y'know the first-ones send some of their young ones to learn to read and write too. You'll meet some, probly some of Jimbo's people too. But Mrs H don't teach no more herself. And the teachers and the learners all help with the gardens and animals.'

Kam looked around him. 'Elly thought about bein a teacher here at Mrs H's. Then she met Jimbo.'

Nox couldn't bring himself to care about Elly's concerns. He was fascinated by the things spread throughout the rooms which really were underground as Kam had said, built into the hillside under the bush warming in the early Brisbane summer. Nox hadn't really believed it.

'What about when all this stuff is used up?'

'Mrs H always said if you want to survive, better hook up with one of the first-ones, the bush people. Least, if you want to have kids that'll grow up. I think that's why Elly took up with Jimbo, she knows her baby'll be safe in the bush in a mergency.'

Nox saw that Kam was searching among the books. 'Are you lookin for somethin special?'

'Yeah. One that tells about makin sick animals better. Elly reckons Mum said I'd be good at that. I think so too. I already look after them, but I can learn more about it.'

Nox was impressed. 'Like a proper animal doctor.'

'Yep. Mum talked to Mrs H about me comin here before she died, when she came to bring Elly home. I gotta talk to Elly about comin to stay again, like you are this time.'

Nox was pleased to think Kam might return to stay, but at the moment he was occupied, wandering about, peering into boxes, going on tiptoe to look on high shelving, opening cupboards.

'We got nothin' like this.'

'Course not. Mrs H's been collectin since before the dust.'

'No, not all the stuff. I mean the cupboards and the shelves, even the house. I never seen a house like this before. I only seen ones made of rough logs and bits and pieces of wood. And look at these shelves and the tables and the chairs, all the wood is smooth and shiny. How does that happen?'

'If you stay, Nox, you can find out.' Mrs H had come into the room behind them. 'Why don't we sit down and have a talk?'

Mrs H's voice was thin and quavery and her steps uncertain, but her pale gaze was as sharp as a quill on an echidna. He and Kam found seats at a long table, half of it covered by books, and Mrs H joined them.

He started stroking the wood of the table, only half-aware of doing so. The grain was clearly visible through the lustre on the wood's surface, whatever it was, and the wood was so smooth and inviting to the touch Nox couldn't resist it.

'Nox?'

Nox realised Kam had said his name twice.

'Nox?'

This time it was Mrs H saying his name. Nox shook himself and looked at the old lady. Mrs H.

'Mrs H,' he heard himself ask, 'what's your proper name?'

'Nox!'

The old lady smiled and put a shaky hand out towards Kam. 'It's all right, Kam, I don't mind. Nox, have you heard the name Weller?

Nox was uncertain. He looked at Kam who just gazed back. 'Weller. I think I have.' He frowned, gazing at the shiny table. 'Wasn't Weller a really bad bloke who did something horrible? I'm not sure.'

Looking down at her papery hands, Mrs H nodded, 'Yes. My name is Weller, Harriet Weller. My husband was Randall Weller and we had two sons and three grandchildren, but they're all gone.'

Nox was staring at the old lady during this gloomy recital. He looked now at Kam who raised a hand slightly as though to say *there's more yet.*

'Um,' Nox mumbled, 'sad.'

Mrs H nodded. Her light blue eyes were sort of cloudy but still bright. 'You've heard the name Weller because it was a certain chemist named Weller, here in Brisbane,'—like the river, Brizba—'who started the end of civilisation, the end of the old days.'

Nox looked from her to Kam and back again. Kam was watching Mrs H attentively. This is the story Kam wouldn't tell Nox. It was Mrs H's story, but Kam had said it was their story too.

'My husband created an enzyme that worked magic in car engines. You won't understand the value of that, but there used to be millions of cars and they all used petrol. But bacteria or a virus or something infected the petrol and before long it began to affect the metal containing the petrol, and from there spread into other metals. Into all metals.'

Mrs H fell silent. The boys stayed quiet, waiting, Nox unsure about some of the words Mrs H was using.

'It started here in Brisbane but it spread all over the world. The virus or infection sort of made all metal sick, and anyone leaving Brisbane carried the virus with them, in the metal at the end of their shoelaces, in the metal that closed their wallets and handbags, in the metal of their jewellery. Slowly everything fell apart and people in cities and towns died because they couldn't breathe the metallic dust that filled the air.

'We went camping, my husband and I, out in the bush. Our children and grandchildren wouldn't come with us, they all died in the city, and we only returned when the air was clear. Our house and garage had collapsed, all our hinges and locks vanished. All that was left of our car were the tyres and the seats and the floor mats.' She shook her head. 'We rebuilt with wood. It was hard.'

She was gazing into a picture only she could see.

'I never saw it happen but I expect planes fell out of the sky, ships sank with all aboard, trains fell apart.' She looked directly at the boys. 'Machinery was destroyed, tractors and tools on farms, things to prepare and package food, all crumbled and crumpled away into powder.'

Mrs H looked around the room, touched the wooden table with stiff deformed fingers.

'For a long, long time, Brisbane had clouds of dust above it from the skyscrapers, the big buildings, that fell, but we had lots of trees to filter the air and we were safe.'

Nox gazed at her intently. Buildings so high they scraped the sky.

Then with sudden briskness she said, 'Kam! Where's the special thing you have for me from Elly?'

'I'll get it!' Nox ran to retrieve Kam's bag from their room. When he returned Kam was telling Mrs H that it really came from his mother.

'Mum always said it had to be kept at the bottom of the wood Chinese box under the bed linen. I remember her sayin' that even though the box once had metal hinges, nothin' metal ever went inside of it.'

Mrs H watched eagerly as Kam opened the canvas bag. From deep within he pulled out a small package wrapped in layers of cloth. He extracted a small object and placed it on Mrs H's open palm. Taking a deep breath, she held it in front of her face. Both boys leaned over the table to look at it. It was about as long as Nox's hand from the tip of his little finger to his wrist, half dark brown with yellow-gold writing or figures on it, the other half a silvery-grey.

'What is it?' he asked Kam, who shrugged.

Then Kam said, '*Shit*, 'scuse me, Mrs H.' He reached into his bag again. 'I'm a galah. I nearly forgot there's a note for you from my mum. She said it had to go with that thing.'

Kam opened up a lined page with handwriting scrawled between the lines. 'Do you want me to read it?' Her nod was distant; she was still holding the strange object, turning it over and over.

'Dear Mrs H, last year Robbo brought me three brass.' At a sound from Mrs H, he said, 'B, R, A, S.'

'Bras. Short for brassieres. Women's underwear.'

The boys looked at each other mystified. Kam went on, '— three bras but they only lasted about ten days. I hope you have better luck with the file. It's been wrapped in layers of clothing at the bottom of a wood trunk. I'm not well, Mrs H. Thanks for looking after my kids. Thanks for everything.'

'What's it mean, about the bras?'

'The metal on the bras crumbled away,' Mrs H said.

'Metal underwear?' Nox couldn't picture it.

Mrs H made a vague gesture across her chest and said, 'For women. For wearing here, to hold things properly in place, closed at the back with metal clips.' She sighed. 'When did your mother write this? What year?'

'Elly told me it was two years ago.'

Nox asked again, 'What is that thing?'

Kam took it on himself to answer when Mrs H stayed quiet, staring down. 'I don't know. Elly wouldn't let me open it, and she said Mum wouldn't let her open it either. Mum told Elly that Mrs H had to be the one to open it.'

Mrs H said, 'It's a nail file, just a simple nail file. It's for filing fingernails, toenails too. Look—'

Mrs H held her left hand in front of her and put her thumb flat against the next finger. With her right hand she brought the nail file to her thumb nail. She started to rub the silvery-grey half across the top of the nail, first one way, then the other, in short light strokes.

Kam asked, 'Can I touch it?' as Nox said, 'But what's it do, Mrs H?'

She gave it to Kam who took it reverently. When she looked at Nox he was alarmed to see that the faded blue of her eyes was awash with tears. She blinked and shook her head a little. 'It's for filing fingernails, Nox, for shaping them and smoothing out rough edges.'

He looked at his own nails. 'Mine break, or I bite them.'

Nox was pleased when Mrs H laughed but he felt his own face react to the return of sadness to her face. She leaned across and took his hands in hers.

'If this metal nail file crumbles away, we'll know that the infection that destroys metal is still active, still alive. It may never be overcome. But if it doesn't crumble at all, it will mean that sooner or later, somewhere in the world, someone will begin manufacturing metal again.'

Nox knew this is all terribly important to her but it didn't mean much to him. Gently retaking possession of his hands, he said, 'But Mrs H, you might miss all that metal stuff, but us, Kam and me, we never known it so we don't miss it.'

'That's true, Nox, very true. But after all the awful things that happened, I would be thrilled if metals can be used again. Metals have been basic to a decent quality of life for centuries and will be again some day. I just hate knowing that it was my husband who accidentally set off the dreadful combination of events that made it all happen.'

Mrs H's quaky voice had firmed up during this speech, but she sounded a bit tearful at the end.

'I don't think it was your husband's fault, Mrs H,' Kam said, handing the nail file back to her. 'Mum always used to say it was an unhappy accident.'

Nox remembered something. 'Hey, Kam, you know Old Ned?'

Kam said, 'Yep,' and turned to Mrs H, 'Old Ned lives out bush, and he's got this stone sharpener and he sharpens our stone tools and bits of concrete, what we use for cutting.'

When Mrs H nodded, Kam said to Nox, 'What about him?'

'He reckons it's all God's fault.'

'Yeah, that's right, he does.'

Mrs H asked, 'Why does he say that?'

'Well, Old Ned said that once he used to be a true believer and he expected to be ruptured away but instead everybody choked to death or starved and he was lucky that he was out in the bush when it happened. So it's God's fault for not rupturing people away like Ned believed he was gunna.'

Nox checked with Kam, who nodded, 'Something like that.'

Mrs H looked as if she was smiling. 'I think he might have said *rapture*, Nox.'

'Could be.'

'Some people used to believe that God would take them to heaven in rapture, in joy and happiness. But that certainly didn't happen. '

Nox didn't care enough to have either rupture or rapture defined, so he switched off when Mrs H started talking to Kam about Elly's baby. Vaguely aware that Mrs H was part of history and that he ought to care more, Nox began gently rubbing the edge of the table, finding the tiny imperfections in the shiny layer that covered the wood. He must ask Mrs H about the furniture. Maybe he could learn to make such beautiful things while he was here.

He looked around the room. Along one long wall were pages like megzine pages, but with just black writing. He went across to study the writing. Kam arrived beside him and read aloud, 'AUSTRALIA QUARANTINED: may be too late for world.' The boys knew about quarantines: chooks had to be quarantined when some got sick.

Kam read, 'DEADLY METAL BLIGHT: unstoppable say UN scientists.'

Before Nox could ask anything, Mrs H said, 'That was right at the end, the end of newspapers, the internet, telephones—I've never known what happened in other countries.'

Nox blinked at the strange words and looked along the wall at some of the other pages. Finding words he couldn't read he muttered, 'I *will* stay. I want to read better and I want to find out what those numbers mean and—'

'What numbers, Nox?' Mrs H was behind him.

'Like 2032, see there, the quarantine page, and I want to learn how to make tables and drawers like these.'

'I want to see if the nail file crumbles or not,' Kam said.

'Me too,' said Mrs H.

5292 words

PUBLICATIONS

P.122 *Mad Melpi* first appeared in 'Imaginary Worlds', an Urchin Press anthology in Sydney, 2016, with the title *Obeying Mad Melphi.*

P.150 *Adara's Secret* was shortlisted for 'Andromeda Spaceways Magazine' in 2021.

ABOUT THE AUTHOR

Frances Goodey

I am a latecomer to publishing my work. At 64, I graduated with a Fine Arts degree, majoring in Creative Writing.

I am the convenor of Quills, the writing group of Ruby Gardens, Eagleby, in Queensland. Since we meet weekly, writing at and between meetings, we all have a wealth of stories and poems completed.

This book, *Glimpses*, contains 100 stories; they are about one-fifth of my growing total. Many of the stories arose in other writing groups in other places and I thank Quills writers for keeping me writing in recent years.

A special note: writers with Aphantasia (please look it up) should take heart from my ‘glimpses’, pun intended.

Manufactured by Amazon.com.au
Sydney, New South Wales, Australia

15376436R00118